MISSION 6

MOON RACER

mars DIARIES

MISSION 6

MOON RACER

SIGMUND BROUWER

TYNDALE House Publishers, INC.
WHEATON, ILLINOIS

Visit Tyndale's exciting Web site at www.tyndale.com

You can contact Sigmund Brouwer through his Web site at
www.coolreading.com

Moon Racer conceived and illustrated by Luke Daab.
Cover Moon Racer modeled in 3-D by Chris Altemeier.

Designed by Justin Ahrens and Ron Kaufmann

Edited by Ramona Cramer Tucker

ISBN 0-8423-4309-1

Printed in the United States of America

07   06   05   04   03   02   01
7   6   5   4   3   2   1

THIS SERIES IS DEDICATED
IN MEMORY OF MARTYN GODFREY.

Martyn, you wrote books that reached all of us kids at heart. You wrote them because you really cared. We all miss you.

CHAPTER 1

Asteroid.

I used to have this picture in my mind that an asteroid collision meant a rock the size of a mountain ramming a planet or moon at full speed. That the impact would have the power of 10 nuclear bombs. That there would be a massive crater and earthquakes and maybe even parts of the planet or moon splitting off to spin back into space.

Not with this asteroid.

At the most, it had been half the size of a pea. Barely more than space dust. If it had been headed toward Earth, the friction of its high-speed entrance into the atmosphere would have burned it in a brief flare of glory. Anyone seeing it from the ground—and they would have, because even a pea-sized asteroid throws a lot of light when it burns— might have wished upon a star.

It had not hit Earth.

It had hit our spaceship, over three-quarters into its 50-million-mile journey from Mars to Earth. It wasn't like running into an iceberg. We hadn't felt the impact inside the ship. But instantly alarm bells had started to clang, waking all nine of us inside and throwing us into emergency mode.

The tiny piece of intergalactic rock had punctured the outer hull, and now valuable oxygen bled into the vacuum of space. Worse, like a tiny stream of water wearing through soggy paper, the hole was growing far too quickly.

It was too dangerous to suit someone up and send him out attached by a safety cable.

Which meant I was the one to step into outer space.

Well, not me. But my robot body, because it didn't need the protective clumsiness of a space suit.

I was actually still inside the ship, my brain hooked up by computer to the robot controls. Everything that the robot body sensed, however, reached me as if it were my own body out there.

The robot body was connected to the ship by a safety cable, and it floated and bobbed as I tried to find the source of the leak at the back part of the hull. The view beyond the ship was incredible. We were headed directly toward the sun and, at some 120 million miles away, it still seemed like the center of the universe.

It did not look yellow. No, human eyes need an atmosphere to filter colors and out here in space, there was no atmosphere. Instead, it was a circle of incredible brightness.

The Earth was close enough now that I could see it clearly too. Not in front of the sun. That would have been like looking into a floodlight and trying to see a marble glued to the bulb. No, the Earth was off to the side of the sun, and it reflected light as purely as the moon on a dark night.

As a backdrop in all directions, millions and millions of tiny pinpricks showed the light of stars and galaxies. It boggled my mind to think that some of those tiny dots were actually clusters of thousands of stars.

"Tyce? Find anything?"

This was my dad's voice coming through the radio. Not that I needed reminding of the urgency of my mission. If the hole in the hull exploded, all of us inside were dead.

"Nothing yet," I said. "Hang on."

Sunlight caught the rounded hull at an angle that showed me a tiny dent in the perfect titanium skin.

"Think I found it," I said. "Just in front of one of the hydrogen tanks."

I heard Dad gasp. "You mean it hits us a couple feet farther back and . . ."

Pressure inside the hydrogen tank was easily 1,000 times higher than pressure inside the spaceship. If the asteroid pea had hit the tank, we would have blown apart into space dust.

"I will be careful," I said. "Promise."

I'd been handling a robot for years, so I wasn't worried about how to move the robot arms and hands and fingers.

What I was worried about was the welding torch in the robot's right hand.

My job was to seal on a square thin sheet of titanium about the size of a human's palm, like slapping a bandage over a cut. Except it wasn't that simple.

In the fingers of my robot's left hand was a thin rod of titanium alloy.

Because it wasn't pure titanium, it melted at a slightly lower temperature than titanium. I needed to touch the rod and the flame of the welding torch together at the edge of the titanium patch, then melt the tip of the rod so that liquid titanium alloy dribbled over the edge of the patch. As the titanium alloy cooled and solidified again, it would form a seal. Almost like using a glue gun. Once I'd sealed off all sides of the square patch, my job would be finished.

Trouble was, the welding torch flame generated heat at over 2400° F. And I hadn't used a welding torch much.

In fact, this was only my second time.

My first had been on Mars, under the dome, in practice sessions with my friend Rawling McTigre, the director of the Mars Project. That was over 40 million miles away.

I didn't give myself any more time to worry. This hole had to be sealed. Immediately.

I let myself drift closer to the hull. The robot wheels made a dull clank as they hit the hull. It wasn't a sound that reached the audio components of the robot's body, however. Sound can't travel through a vacuum. Instead, I heard it through the slight vibrations that traveled up the robot body.

I was ready.

The titanium patch had a temporary glue to keep it in place as I welded. I pushed the patch down, and the glue held.

Under the lights of millions of stars I began to weld.

What I couldn't adjust to was the intensity of the flame's light. "Dad," I said into the radio, "you need to roll the ship a little so I am not in the shadows."

The sun was on the other side. Its light would make it easier for me to see what I needed to do.

Seconds later, the ship rolled. Just slightly. In space, it takes too much fuel to overcorrect any sudden movements.

It also takes very little change of direction for the movement to be felt.

The robot body started to slide along the hull.

Without thinking—as if I were in gravity instead of outer space—I put out a hand to balance myself. The robot's right hand. The one with the torch.

The hand hit the hull, and the torch bumped loose.

This wasn't a total disaster. In the floating weightlessness of space, I could catch it before it went another 10 feet.

Except two feet away was the hydrogen tank.

I made a slow-motion grab for the torch, but it flipped end over end, in agonizing slowness, just out of reach.

I could see it happening but was helpless to stop it.

The torch flame touched the side of the hydrogen tank. All 2400° F of flame concentrated on high-pressure gas inside. The metal of the tank glowed briefly.

Silently I screamed. But it was too late.

Before I could think any more thoughts, all existence disappeared in a blinding flash far brighter than any star.

CHAPTER 2

I spoke into darkness. "Dad, I've got a headache."

I could easily picture where I was. In the robot lab on the *Moon Racer* spaceship. The spaceship got its name because when it was first built, people said it would easily outrace the moon, which it could. The lab held a computer and a bed. I was on that bed, where my spine plug was able to make an X-ray wave connection to the computer hard drive.

The real robots—there were two—were stored in a cargo bay that gave them immediate access to the exterior of the ship. Although I had used my robot frequently on the surface of Mars, the only reason the robots would be needed during the *Moon Racer*'s journey to Earth was during an emergency situation.

"Headache?" Dad chuckled. "You're lucky you don't have more than that. Welding torches and high-pressured hydrogen fuel tanks don't make for a good mix. I was monitoring your progress in here. You of all people know that the virtual-reality software doesn't mess around."

I knew that Dad was holding the headset, which he had already removed. It had been blocking all sound from reaching my ears. Arms at my side, I was still strapped to the laboratory bed and needed him to remove the blindfold and straps.

"On the trip to Earth—I mean the real trip to Earth—the chances of hitting an asteriod are one in billions, right?" I said defensively. "And then the chances of a puncture near the fuel tank are . . . are . . ."

Dad removed my blindfold, and I blinked a couple of times. His smiling face loomed down at me. He had blondish hair, like mine, and a large frame. I only hope that someday I'll grow up to be as big as he is.

"Tyce," he answered, his face now serious, "that's the whole point of these virtual-reality training programs. To prepare you for any situation, no matter how unlikely. If for some reason—no matter how unlikely—you are called for any duty, you can't afford mistakes."

He unstrapped me. I sat up.

"I'm sorry," I said. I meant it. Dad was 100 percent correct. And, after all, he had to be. He was the *Moon Racer*'s pilot, the one we all trusted with our lives.

"Could you let me try another run this afternoon?"

His smile returned. "That would take you away from your mathematics, wouldn't it?"

"Much more important to know how to save a spaceship than it is to deal with logarithmic derivatives and triple integrals."

"Perhaps," he said. His grin grew wider. "But I was thinking of your friend Ashley. I was getting the impression that she enjoyed the chance to do schoolwork with you."

I coughed. Ashley and I were roughly the same age. She'd arrived on the last shuttle to Mars in June and now was on her way back to Earth with me. The two of us were the only ones under the age of 25, and we liked to hang out together. "She just needs a little help, that's all."

Dad laughed. He unstrapped me from the bed. I pushed off and began to float in the weightlessness. This was one thing I loved about space travel. I didn't need my wheel-chair.

"Don't let her fool you, Tyce. I've seen the background report on her. The worst grade she ever got in math was a 95 percent." Dad rubbed my hair. "And your best grade has been . . . ?"

"So I don't like math that much," I said.

I reached for my comp-board. It was floating beside the bed where I had left it before the virtual-reality robot ses-sion. Dad had asked me to bring it with but hadn't told me why yet.

Comp-board was the term used for keyboard-computer, a portable computer with the screen attached directly to the back of the keyboard. The hard drive was embedded in the left-hand side of the keyboard, with discports on the right-hand side. When I was finished with the computer, all I had to do was fold the keyboard in half, then fold that against the back of the screen, and it would become a small rectan-gle about the size of a book. Back at the dome, the comp-board actually docked into my desktop computer, letting me access the comp-board hard drive but giving me access to a bigger screen.

"She's really that good in math?" I asked.

"Uh-huh."

"If she's so good, then why would she always ask me to help her?"

To give me free use of my hands, I attached the folded-up comp-board to a latch on my belt. I grabbed a hand-hold—they were placed all through the ship to give passengers a way to travel in the weightlessness—and followed Dad out of the robot lab.

"Where are we headed?" I queried. Dad and I traveled down the inner corridor of the *Moon Racer.*

"I need to tweak some of the autopilot controls," Dad answered. "Our mainframe computer has been a little cranky lately. But we need to make a quick stop first."

"Where?"

"I know you're trying to change the subject," Dad laughed. "Let's get back to math."

"Math?" I tried to sound innocent.

"She wants *you* to learn the math better," Dad answered. "Whatever lies ahead of you, Tyce, I'm guessing it will involve exploration of the solar system. You're going to need advanced calculus to get any kind of education that allows for space travel."

"If she wants me to learn better, why doesn't *she* teach *me?*"

Dad laughed again. "She is. Sometimes the best way to learn is by figuring something out for yourself, then teaching it to someone else."

"Oh."

"She might have another reason too."

"What's that?" I asked Dad.

"All I'm saying is that she sure seems to smile a lot when she's around you."

"Huh?"

"You figure it out." He stopped in front of a closed hatch that led to a private bunker. The hatch was a circular opening, twice as wide as Dad's shoulders. The "door" to the hatch slid open or shut by entering a code into one of the small keypads—one on the outside and one on the inside.

Dad began to punch the five-digit code.

"Hey," I said, "this is Blaine Steven's bunker."

"I know," Dad said. "He wants to talk to you."

"Me? He's already tried to kill me three different times."

CHAPTER 3

The hatch door slid open, and my heart started to pound.

After all, Blaine Steven had been the first director of the Mars Project—before he almost got everyone under the dome killed in the oxygen crisis. And then he'd been part of a plot to take over the dome while the present director, my friend Rawling, and I had been off on a mission on the planet's surface. The guy couldn't be trusted. So why would my dad want me to talk with him?

"I think you should speak to him," Dad said quietly. "He's been asking for you specifically. And this is after five and a half months of refusing to speak to anyone on the *Moon Racer*. He also asked that you take your comp-board."

I shook my head. This all seemed so unreal. "You'll wait for me?" I asked Dad anxiously.

"I'll be right here," he said.

"I'm not sure I want to be alone with him," I said nervously.

"He insisted," Dad said. "And he won't be able to do anything to you as long as you stay out of his reach.

Remember that. And all you need to do is yell, and I'll be there."

"Thanks," I said. But I still didn't like the idea.

I floated into Blaine Steven's prison bunker. Dad shut the hatch behind me. The clank echoed. It felt like I had been shut into prison myself.

With only a couple of weeks of the journey left, why did Blaine Steven want to see me? And why did he want me to bring my comp-board?

"Hello, Tyce."

The man on the far side of the bunker wore the regulation blue jumpsuit, with one difference. A wide metal band circled his waist. This band was attached to the wall by a short length of cable. It gave him just enough room to reach his E-book and other possessions and take care of his personal needs. Anywhere else but in weightlessness, a leash like this would have been cruel punishment.

"Hello," I answered. Without friendliness. This man had tried to do a lot of damage to the Mars Project. And to me.

"Thanks for coming," the silver-haired man with cold blue eyes said. He looked like a dignified judge. But I knew he used this respectable appearance to fool people.

I shrugged.

"I can understand that you don't feel much like talking with me," he said.

I remembered what it had been like the other times we spoke. When he was director. In his office. Under the dome. On Mars. Where he had treated me like a blob of mud to be scraped off his shoe.

I shrugged again.

"And that's all right," he said. "I can do most of the talking, if you like."

Steven put his finger to his mouth as if he were silencing me. It didn't make sense. I was already silent.

He pointed at my computer and gestured for me to give it to him. I shook my head no. How could I trust him with it?

"It is very important that we talk," he said pleasantly. As he spoke, he acted as if he were typing on a keyboard. "I hope you understand that," he said in the same pleasant tone. He put his hands together as if he were begging. Then he pretended to keyboard again.

"And I also hope you will feel free to say anything you want to me." Except his actions showed the opposite. He violently shook his head from side to side, mouthing the word *no*. He pointed to the walls around him and pointed to his ears.

Despite my intense dislike for him, I was curious. Did he mean that I shouldn't speak freely because the walls were listening?

He made the same begging motion as before and pointed at my computer again.

As crazy as this all was, I made a decision to find out what he wanted. To play his game, if even for a minute. After all, I knew I could always yell for help and Dad would be there in a flash. "I'm not sure I want to talk to you," I said. But I unfolded the keyboard, popped the screen up, and powered the comp-board. The screen brightened. I opened a new file in a word processing program. "What is there to talk about?"

Making sure I didn't get near Steven, I pushed the comp-board ahead. It floated toward him. He smiled with gratitude.

"I want to ask you about your faith," Steven said. He brought his knees up to give him a support for the comp-board. "Spending all this time alone in prison has given me a lot of time to think."

"Faith?" I asked, shocked.

"I've been thinking about my life. What I've done with it. And what might happen if I die."

This was the last thing I'd expected to talk about with Blaine Steven, the man who didn't seem to have a conscience. Who'd been willing to kill a couple hundred people under the dome to save some key scientists and their illegal experiment.

"I can see the surprise on your face," he said. "Take some time to think about your answer."

He put his head down and began to type frantically, humming loudly to cover the sound of his fingers on the keyboard.

When he finished, he pushed the comp-board in my direction. It slowly drifted through the bunker and I reached for it before it floated past me.

He put his finger in front of his mouth again. But it was a warning I didn't need. Not after reading the first words he had typed onto the screen.

Don't say anything. I am sure there are listening devices in this bunker.

I lifted my head and nodded at Steven.

I read more.

I have vital information about the rebels who are trying to destroy the dome and take over the World United Federation. But I will not give out this information unless I know I will be protected. Which includes your silence. Do you agree?

I typed, *I will remain silent in here.*

I wasn't going to make much more of a promise until I knew more. Especially with a man I'd never liked, a man who couldn't be trusted. I pushed the comp-board toward him.

"Faith is important to you, isn't it?" he said in the same pleasant tone. I knew he was speaking for the benefit of the listening device. If there really was one.

"I can't tell you I have all the answers," I said. "But, yes, it is important."

As I spoke, he quickly read my answer and typed one of his own, humming the entire time.

He pushed the comp-board back to me.

"I am beginning to see that faith is the most important thing a person can have," Blaine Steven said. "And I would like it if you visited me more often so that we could talk about it."

I hardly heard him as my eyes scanned the screen.

You know that Dr. Jordan and I are part of the Terratakers rebel group and worked together in the dome to overthrow the World United's control of Mars. But there is someone else of greater power we report to. And far more hidden. Even from me. And I now believe this mastermind is on this ship. I can hear strange things happening through the wall. I think Dr. Jordan is working with the mastermind. They want to make sure that I do not survive the trip to Earth.

Through the wall. Dr. Jordan's prison bunker was on the other side of this one.

I typed a question in response, *Who is the other person that you say is the mastermind behind the rebels?*

Although I moved closer to Blaine Steven to give him the comp-board, I still made sure I was out of his reach. I waited as he typed frantically.

He gave me the comp-board.

If I knew who it was, I would tell you. My best guess

about their plan is an explosive device. But don't limit the search for that. If you see anything unusual, be suspicious. Find a way to stop them. I will keep my other secrets until I'm sure I can trade them for my freedom. Or my life.

I typed two words. *Explosive device?*

This was Blaine Steven's answer on the screen: *I distinctly heard the word bomb. Which terrifies me. And should terrify you. Because I am not the only one they want dead.*

CHAPTER 4

"What are you doing!"

Stuck against the far wall of one of the spaceship's bunker areas, I had little room to move. The bunker was little more than a bed on a large shelf, with other smaller shelves below. Each of those shelves had loose netting in front so that the objects on them would not float out.

"What are you doing!" came the angry response again. The man who floated head first in the hatchway to the bunker wore the regulation blue jumpsuit. But all I could see were his head and shoulders since the rest of his body hung out in the corridor. I knew he didn't look regulation in any other way. His upper body was an upside-down triangle, his waist narrow and his shoulders and chest so heavily muscled that he barely fit into the hatchway. His neck seemed as wide as his head. Because he cut his dark hair so short, the first thing you noticed about his square face was his ears, which stuck straight out from his head. Not that anyone would ever mention it to him.

Turning my head to look at him was an awkward move, considering I was on my back. Or on my side. Or upside down. It's hard to tell in the weightlessness of interplanetary travel since all positions feel the same. But in relationship to the ceiling, I clung to a handhold bar on the wall, with a vacuum tube floating beside me. So I probably looked like a fly, with my legs tucked beneath me in the cramped quarters of the bunker.

What made me look like a thief, however, was the fact that I had undone the netting of his shelves.

"What are you doing!" Lance Evenson repeated one more time. As his body showed, he was a workout freak and had a reputation for using his size to frighten people. It worked. I *was* frightened at his anger. "And tell me why you're in my bunker area without my permission!"

I wasn't going to tell him I was looking for a bomb. No, when Dad had sent me out with a vacuum tube, he'd been very clear we needed to keep it a secret. One, as Dad had warned, we did not want to let the traitor know we knew about the bomb. And two, we didn't want to panic all the others.

"I'm . . . I'm . . . cleaning," I said. I pointed at the vacuum tube. It was about as long and as wide as my arm, with a powerful little motor hidden inside. It was designed to pick up crumbs and dust that hung in the air.

"I can see you're cleaning," he answered angrily. "What I want to know is why you have invaded my privacy and what you expect to clean among my personal possessions on the shelf."

Although his official title was chief computer technician, Lance Evenson's job was considered to be far, far more crucial than the duties of most tekkies. Computers were the lifeblood of space exploration. In the dome on Mars. And on a spaceship. Power equipment, machines, engines—all depended on computers. Positional information and the calculation of space orbits depended on computers. All communications depended on computers. And all those computers depended on the chief computer technician for maintenance and repairs. No one reached the status of chief computer technician without years of training and experience. It was easier to become a doctor than a chief computer technician. And for good reason. Doctors were responsible for one life at a time. A chief computer technician was responsible for every life under the dome. Or on a spaceship.

"My dad asked me to vacuum everywhere," I said. "He told me it's part of regular duties on a long flight like ours. Good as the filters are, he wants to stay on top of the dust and particles so there's absolutely no chance of clogging anything important."

"Humph," Lance said. "That's news to me. I don't remember doing it on my trip to Mars."

Which had been nearly 15 Earth years ago. Lance had been on the Mars Dome since it had been established. This was his first trip back to Earth. Having a man of his knowledge and expertise to help if anything went wrong was fortunate for the rest of us.

"News to me too," I answered. "I'd rather be in a simulation software game right now. But this is my first flight, and how can I disagree with my dad? Especially because he's the pilot."

I said that as a way to remind Lance that he, too, had to follow the pilot's orders. Chief computer technician or not, in space the first rule was that the pilot had total authority.

"Fine, then," Lance said. He pulled himself through the hatchway and, with a slight push, sent himself toward me. He put out an arm and stopped himself against the wall beside me. "Give me the vacuum tube. I'll take care of it."

"I don't mind doing it," I said, trying to shrink back from

the closeness of his large body. "I'm nearly done in here anyway."

"I don't care. I want you out of my bunker."

"Yes, sir," I said.

I pushed off the wall, toward the hatch. I grabbed the handhold bars on each side.

As I began to pull my body forward, like a worm about to squeeze out of a hole, Lance's voice stopped me.

"Pilot's order or not," Lance said harshly, "I don't want to catch you in here again. If there's something you need in my bunker, you talk to *me* first. And I'll be telling the same thing to your father. Got that?"

"Got it," I said.

"Good. Then get out of my sight. And close the hatch door behind you."

I pushed my head through the hatchway and looked both directions up and down the corridor. Although there were only nine people on the ship, we'd all learned early to check before shooting out of our bunkers. Weightlessness or not, collisions still hurt.

Once the rest of my body was out of the hatch, I flipped over, like a fish doing a somersault in water. I secured the hatch.

I grabbed the nearest handhold bar and shoved off to find Dad.

He'd want to know about this.

Because I was willing to bet a lot of money that Lance Evenson was hiding something.

CHAPTER 5

Of the entire ship, my favorite area was the navigation cone, which formed the nose of the ship. For two reasons. One, the telescope was located there, and I'd spent every evening that I could at the telescope under the dome on Mars. And two, because standing in the cone was like being perched in outer space.

The cone was the only place with a view. The rest of the ship behind it was made of a titanium alloy, and the bunkers and work areas had no windows. They were lit by the pale whiteness of low-energy argon tubes inset into the walls and activated by nearby movement.

The cone sat in front, where it looked like an awkward addition. But because there's no air in space, or any gravity to pull a structure apart, the ship was designed much differently than if it had to fly in an atmosphere.

Essentially the entire ship was a large circular tube, moving sideways through the vacuum of space. The outer part of this large tube held the docking port, two emergency escape ports, an exercise room, all the passenger bunkers, and work-area compartments. The inner part of the circle formed a corridor, which we traveled by grabbing handholds

MOON RACER

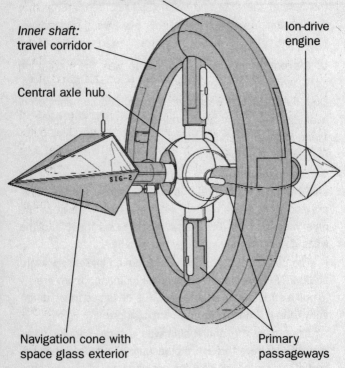

Outer perimeter: docking port, bunkers, work areas, kitchen, exercise room, and emergency escape ports

Inner shaft: travel corridor

Central axle hub

Ion-drive engine

Navigation cone with space glass exterior

Primary passageways

and pushing forward or backward, entering the bunkers or work areas through circular hatches with slide-away covers. From this corridor, four main hatches led to tubes that extended downward like spokes and met at a center hub. From this center hub one short tube led backward to the pyramid-shaped, ion-drive engine. Another short hub led forward to the pyramid-shaped navigation cone.

Here, in the navigation cone, the titanium structure of the rest of the ship had been replaced by material that looked and functioned like glass but was thousands of times stronger and more expensive. All of the walls of the pyramid were made of this space glass, including the floor. The computer and control console sat on this glass floor, as did the pilot's seat. That's why I liked it so much. Pushing from the hub into the navigation cone made it seem like a person was floating directly into clear outer space. This sensation frightened some people, but because in gravity situations I spent so much time in a wheelchair, I loved the illusion of freedom.

This time, however, pushing from the confined tube of the hub into the navigation cone to visit my dad gave me little pleasure.

Not with the news I had to deliver.

"Nothing," I told him. "I found nothing unusual except one cranky chief computer technician."

I explained to Dad what had happened during my search.

Sitting before a computer screen and the ship's controls, Dad leaned back, hands locked behind his head. His face showed little expression as he listened.

"What do you think?" I asked when I finished. "Sounds suspicious, doesn't it?"

"First, we don't know for sure that there is a bomb or a plot. Remember who the information is coming from. Second, even if there is a plot, I highly doubt Lance Evenson could be part of a master plot like this. And even if he did intend to hide a bomb, we'd never find it. He's brilliant."

"But he made it clear he didn't want me in his bunker. That must mean something."

Dad grinned. "It means he's one of the most stubborn, opinionated, and cranky men I know. If you'd been in there trying to give him money, he still would have kicked you out. Just because you didn't ask permission to go into his bunker ahead of time."

I wanted to protest. But before I could say anything, Ashley arrived, bobbing through the air, holding a vacuum tube identical to mine.

I was still getting used to it, watching the way that all of us moved in weightless conditions. Whichever direction a person pushed, he or she would continue to move in that direction until hitting something, grabbing something to stop, or pushing off in a different direction.

Most bizarre of all, however, was what happened to liquids that spilled. In gravity situations, of course, all of it fell straight down and splattered. Not on a spaceship. Droplets would move slowly in all directions, in big and little blobs, and with enough time and patience you could herd all the droplets by capturing them in a container. (This made bathroom arrangements very interesting.)

"Mr. Sanders," Ashley said after her quick hello to both of us, "are you sure this isn't some kind of trick that you and Rawling decided to play on me and Tyce?"

Dad raised an eyebrow. I admired the move and had been practicing it myself. But only when no one was around.

"What I mean," she said, "is that maybe this is a way to get us to clean the ship. You know, getting us into every corner and hidden space with a vacuum tube."

Dad shook his head with a sad smile. "I wish it was."

Ashley sighed. She floated on her side in midair, as if she were on an invisible sofa. "I was afraid of that."

"Nothing, huh?" I asked. I was on my stomach in midair, facing her and Dad. The constant hum of the air circulators surrounded us, as the filters removed carbon dioxide and replaced it with oxygen generated from special tanks.

"Nothing. I'm scared of finding it. And scared of *not* finding it," she said, pushing back the short, black hair that floated around her face.

I knew exactly what she meant. We absolutely had to find the bomb to have a chance of surviving this trip. But if we did find it, would we discover that it couldn't be moved or safely disarmed?

"I'll agree with you," Dad answered intensely. Then he frowned. "What's worse, I'm not sure we have much time."

Dad unlocked his hands and leaned forward. Normally any movement like that in weightlessness meant he would keep falling forward unless he grabbed at the armrests of his chair. But because pilots needed to be stable during any maneuvers, small Velcro patches on the seat of his jumpsuit kept him attached to his chair.

"It's like this," he said. "It's unlikely that whoever planted the bomb is suicidal. Agreed?"

"Agreed," Ashley and I said together.

"Which means he is not going to explode the bomb unless he can get away."

"Agreed," we said again.

"So think about our escape pods."

I was beginning to understand. There were nine of us on the *Moon Racer*. Each of the escape pods was capable of holding 10 people, supplying them with enough food and water and oxygen for three weeks. The *Moon Racer* carried two escape pods because it often had up to 20 passengers.

"If he's going to blow up the *Moon Racer*," I said, "he'll use the space pod to escape first. That means he needs to be less than three weeks away from any shuttle that can pick him up."

"Exactly," Dad said. "If I were him, I'd use the *Moon Racer*'s direction and momentum. Once we were three weeks from arrival, I'd eject in the direction of Earth and turn on my distress signal in the escape pod. Any one of dozens of Earth-Moon shuttles would be able to pick up the pod once it's within orbit range."

Ashley's lips tightened and her almond eyes flashed. "And we are now within the escape pods' range of Earth."

"Give or take a couple of days," Dad said. "The important thing is to keep this among the three of us and to find different ways to search."

I knew what I'd be doing. Watching Lance Evenson. And I had an idea how to do it.

I caught Dad frowning at me, as if he were reading my mind.

I was wrong.

"Just had an idea," he said. "Did either of you check our escape pods for a bomb?"

My eyes widened. "Hadn't thought of it."

"I'll check them both," Dad said quickly, as he turned on the autopilot controls and then got out of his seat. "If the bomb is in one, he must intend to use the other."

"Finding it in an escape pod would solve the problem, wouldn't it?" I said. "If we can't disarm the bomb, we'll just eject the pod into space and not care where it blows up."

Great solution. Except, as it turned out, I was wrong about that too.

CHAPTER 6

"You know what's weird?" Ashley asked me.

Except for the usual background humming of the *Moon Racer*'s air circulation units, it was quiet. She and I were at our usual early evening meeting place. In the *Moon Racer*'s observation quarters.

It was the same size as the robot lab, but there was no computer or X-ray receiver. Instead, a telescope tube fit through the upper panels and extended beyond the ship. Six months to Mars and six months back is a lot of travel time, and Earth scientists use a lot of the recorded information from this telescope. After all, there's no atmosphere to interfere with the view and the camera shots and real-time visuals from this telescope are amazing.

I could, and did, spend hours here, looking at clusters of galaxies and supernovas and all the different planets of the solar system. It never failed to stagger me, wondering where all this beauty came from. It never failed to lead me to thoughts about God.

"I'll bite," I said. I was floating upside down beneath the telescope tube, staring at Mars, wondering what Mom was doing right now, back on Mars. And if Rawling had started a new project without me. The swirls of red made me home-sick. "What's weird?"

"Just yesterday, Dr. Jordan wanted to ask me questions."

"What!" I would have jumped if there was any gravity. I switched my attention from Mars to Ashley.

"Don't look at me like that. It's not that big a deal. I was going down the corridor and Luke Daab was doing some maintenance work on the hatch door to Dr. Jordan's prison bunker. Luke said Dr. Jordan wanted to ask me a question. I didn't even go inside. I just stuck my head through the hatch. Dr. Jordan was cabled to the wall, of course. And Luke Daab was right beside me, so I knew I was safe."

"What did he ask?" I didn't feel any better because of what I'd heard. Blaine Steven was bad enough, but compared to the evil Dr. Jordan, Blaine seemed like an innocent baby.

"About my escape. You know, the Hammerhead."

I knew. The Hammerhead was an experimental space torpedo that Ashley and I were each capable of controlling remotely through robot virtual reality. It was the reason Ashley had been sent to Mars. Jordan's plan had been to test the Hammerhead where no one on Earth would be able to see or understand its military power. But at the last minute, Ashley had found a way to prevent the test from happening, since she didn't want anyone on Earth ever threatened by it.

"Did you tell him?"

"Not a chance. You know it makes me sick to even think of him. I hope he wonders for the rest of his life. Especially since you know how easy it was."

I did. The test had taken place from a shuttle that orbited Mars. Just before the test began, Ashley had loaded a spare space suit into the Hammerhead. Because only the dark helmet and visor were visible to us inside the shuttle, it looked like she was at the controls. Instead, she had remained inside the cargo bay, speaking to us as if she were actually on the space torpedo. She controlled the first part of the Hammerhead's flight, long enough to set its course for impact on the distant moon. It fooled all of us, including Dr. Jordan, into thinking she had died during the crash. After the shuttle landed on Mars, she sneaked out of the cargo bay unnoticed and hid in the dome until it was finally safe to appear again.

"Oh. Was that all he wanted?"

"That was his only question."

"You're right," I said. "That *is* weird."

I should have given it more thought. Dr. Jordan didn't do anything without a reason. But I noticed the look on Ashley's face. She was scared.

"It'll be all right," I said.

"How do you know what I'm thinking?"

"You're thinking about the others in the experimental group." The kids that Ashley and I were supposed to try to find. That was why we were headed back to Earth.

She gave me a small smile. "You know me pretty well."

Ashley was part of a small group of Earth kids who had been operated on to be able to handle robot controls remotely. Dr. Jordan had forced her to go to Mars with a simple and effective threat. If Ashley didn't do exactly as she was told—including maintaining the pretense that she was his daughter—the kids in the experimental group would be killed. That's why she'd made it look like the Hammerhead failure killed her.

"It'll be OK," I said. "Dr. Jordan and Blaine Steven are military prisoners. Word was sent from Mars to keep that highly confidential. Those kids will be all right. I mean, that's why you and I are going back to Earth. To break them loose. They'll be exactly where you left them."

Which was some sort of hidden retreat in the Arizona desert. Once the *Moon Racer* reached the Earth orbit, we would be shuttled to the surface of the planet. After a week to get used to the gravity, Dad would lead us to the retreat and Ashley would show him and other soldiers the entrance. The plan had full military approval.

"Tyce, those were my friends. All of us have been together, training in virtual reality, as long as we can remember. If my actions hurt them, I'd never forgive myself."

As she spoke, she unconsciously touched the silver cross on a chain around her neck. It was an earring, and it matched the cross around my neck, which she'd given me once as a friendship gift.

A thought hit. "You know what else is weird?" I asked.

"What?"

"I've never asked you where you got the silver crosses from. I'd be surprised if one of the rebel leaders who guarded your experimental group gave them to you. . . ."

Another smile from her, this one sad. "They're from my parents. At least, that's what I was told. I was just a baby when they died in a car crash. That's all that I ever had of them. Not even a photo."

Her sad smile didn't change. "That's why I ended up in the experimental group. Because I was an orphan. Like all the others. There was nobody around to wonder where we went or to care what happened to us."

She was thinking about them again. I could tell by her face.

"Really, Ashley," I said softly, "it will be all right."

I didn't add my next thought.

If we make it to Earth.

CHAPTER 7

It was late at night. At least, it was late in the 24-hour schedule that all of us followed. Day and night didn't really exist on the spaceship. We were headed toward the sun, not orbiting around it, so we really didn't have a day or night.

I floated beside my bed, sitting in a cross-legged position with my comp-board on my lap. I stared at the unfolded screen. Over the last few months of travel—because not much new happened from day to day—I had not spent much time on the comp-board adding to my Mars diary entries.

Part of it was because I didn't want to remind myself of the homesickness I felt whenever I couldn't fall asleep quickly.

Like now, reading one of my first entries.

A little over two weeks ago, I was on Mars. Under the dome. Living life in a wheelchair. I'd been born there, and the most I had ever traveled in any direction was 200 miles. Then, with the suddenness of a lightning bolt, I discovered I would be returning to

Earth with Dad as he piloted this spaceship on the three-year round-trip to Earth and back to Mars. Although the actual legs of the journey only take six months to get there and six months to get back, the planets' orbits have to be aligned correctly in order to make the trip. And that takes three years.

I'd been dreaming of Earth for years.

After all, I was the only human in the history of mankind who had never been on the planet. I'd only been able to watch it through the telescope and wonder about snowcapped mountains and blue sky and rain and oceans and rivers and trees and flowers and birds and animals.

Earth.

When Rawling had told me I was going to visit the Earth, I'd been too excited to sleep. Finally, I'd be able to see all the things I'd only read about under the cramped protection of the Mars Dome, where it never rained, the sky outside was the color of butterscotch, and the mountains were dusty red.

But when it came time to roll onto the shuttle that would take us to the *Moon Racer*, waiting in orbit around Mars, I had discovered an entirely new sensation. Homesickness. Mars—and the dome— was all I knew.

Dozens of technicians and scientists had been there when we left, surprising me by their cheers and affection. Rawling had been there, the second-to-last person to say good-bye, shaking my hand gravely, then leaning forward to give me a hug.

And the last person?

That had been Mom, biting her lower lip and

blinking back tears. It hurt so much seeing her sad—and feeling my own sadness. I'd nearly rolled my wheelchair right back away from the shuttle. Three years—at that moment—seemed like an eternity. I knew that if an accident happened anywhere along the 100 million miles of travel to Earth and back, I might never see her again. Mom must have been able to read my thoughts because she'd leaned forward to kiss me and told me to not even dare think about staying. She'd whispered that although she'd miss me, she knew that I was in God's hands, so I wouldn't be alone. She said she was proud of me for taking this big step, and that she'd pray every day for my and Dad's safe return.

The first few nights on the spaceship had not been easy. All alone in my bunker I had stared upward in the darkness for hours and hours, surprised at how much the sensation of homesickness could fill my stomach.

Who would think that a person could miss a place that would kill you if you walked outside without a space suit. . . .

My comp-board bogged down. The arrow kept scrolling down the page, but the letters on the screen lagged behind.

I stopped. This was puzzling. Except for the short time this afternoon with Blaine Steven, this had also happened the last time I used my comp-board. I'd even asked Lance Evenson to check it then, but he'd said it was my imagination.

Except this was definitely not my imagination.

I scrolled farther and finally got to the end of all that I

had written. As I began to keyboard a new entry, describing the events of this day, the comp-board just as mysteriously began to work at its normal speed.

That was about the only good thing about this bomb threat. It took my mind off how badly I still missed Mom and everyone else on Mars.

I stopped keyboarding again and let my thoughts drift off. I was tempted to fold the comp-board right now and try to sleep again, but I knew that once I closed my eyes, my mind would go right back to wondering about the bomb. Would I have any time to realize what was happening when it exploded? How might it feel to get sucked into the vacuum of outer space? And—

Stop! I told myself.

I focused on the keyboard and began to type again.

> So who might be the "mastermind" that Blaine Steven told me about? That is, if he wasn't lying to me for some reason. And considering his past record, that's a good possibility. . . .
>
> And is the mastermind really on the *Moon Racer*? There aren't that many people on board.
>
> There's me, of course, and Dad and Ashley. Lance Evenson, the chief computer technician. Luke Daab, a maintenance engineer who helped maintain the dome's mechanical equipment during his 15 years on Mars. Susan Fielding, a genetic scientist who only spent three years on Mars. And Jack Tripp, a mining engineer who was returning with a couple tons of rock samples.
>
> There were also two prisoners. Blaine Steven, the ex-director of the dome. And Dr. Jordan, who

had arrived with Ashley on Mars only three months before leaving again on this ship.

Nine altogether. And if one of them . . .

I stopped typing again.

I couldn't help but wonder if Blaine Steven had been telling the truth. Maybe he just wanted to make trouble. I wouldn't put it past him.

But if someone had actually planted a bomb, my first guess, of course, was Lance Evenson. But somehow I didn't think it would be that simple. And it would be dumb to make that assumption without at least considering if it could be anyone else.

If Blaine Steven and Dr. Jordan hadn't been securely sealed in their bunkers, both of them would have been prime suspects. They'd been working together on Mars for a rebel group on Earth and had nearly succeeded in destroying the whole Project. But neither had been able to leave their bunkers, and it would be impossible for either to reach an escape pod. So it couldn't be Steven or Jordan.

Luke Daab? He was a skinny, redheaded guy with a beach-ball belly and a nervous laugh. He chewed his fingernails badly too. I couldn't imagine him trying to pull off something like this.

Susan Fielding—chubby with blonde hair—never spoke above a whisper. Although she was older than Dad, she was smaller than Ashley and never went anywhere on the ship without an E-book in her hands or tucked under an arm. I couldn't picture her as the traitor either.

Maybe Jack Tripp, though. He and Dad were about the same age and the same size. Jack had a big red nose, twitchy red eyebrows to match his wiry red hair, and a loud laugh, usually at his own jokes, which weren't that funny.

The trouble with trying to guess, I realized, was that any guess I made was based on appearance only. I didn't really know much else about them.

I looked at my computer screen, barely focusing on the words I'd already written. Then I thought of something as I stared at my diary entry.

Yes! That was it!

Ashley and I could interview everybody on this ship. We could write about this trip as a school project or even for an E-magazine. Some Web site somewhere would love to have an article about two kids traveling from Mars to Earth. That would be the excuse Ashley and I would use to ask everyone on board more about themselves.

But we'd have to find the traitor sometime in the next few days.

Great as the idea was, I knew I should clear it with Dad first. This, I figured, was as good a time as any to go over and talk to him about it.

I folded up the computer and placed it behind the netting of the shelf beneath my bed. Scooting out the hatch, I maneuvered my way down the corridor to Dad's hatch.

I knocked first, keeping a tight grip on a nearby handhold so that when my knuckles hit his hatch, the counterforce wouldn't float me backward.

"Yes?" He answered immediately from the other side.

"It's me."

I heard the *blip-blip-blip-blip-blip* as he entered his code into the keypad. The hatch door slid open with a hiss.

"Come on in," he said.

I did. He closed the hatch behind me.

I didn't like the expression on his face. "Did I wake you?" I asked.

Usually he was up late, going over ship reports.

"No."

"Good. For a second I thought you were upset."

"I am. But not at you."

Now I really didn't like the expression on his face.

"Tyce," he said gravely, "remember I said I was going to check the escape pods?"

I nodded. "You found the bomb?"

"No, not yet. Worse. Both escape pods have been disabled by a computer malfunction that Lance can't seem to fix. There is no way to safely leave this ship."

CHAPTER 8

"How about one of us uses the ant-bot to find out if Lance Evenson has something hidden in his room?" I asked Ashley.

We were in the exercise room, halfway through the next morning. Ashley sat at a leg-press machine, which, of course, I never used. I sat at a bench-press machine. Sweat covered me. I'd been pushing the weights hard, knowing that once I stepped onto the Earth, my muscles would be working against gravity more than double what I'd faced on Mars.

"I thought of that last night as I was falling asleep," she said. "But I'm not sure we can."

"Why not?"

"I'm not sure it's physically possible on this space-ship."

"We're both wired," I said. Which we were.

For about as long as I could remember, I had been trained in a virtual-reality program. Like the ones on Earth where you put on a surround-sight helmet that gives you a three-dimensional view of a scene on a computer program. The helmet is wired so that when you turn your head, it directs the computer program to shift the scene as if you were there in real life. Sounds come in like real sounds. Because you're wearing a wired jacket and gloves, the arms and hands you see in your surround-sight picture move wherever you move your own arms and hands.

With me, the only difference is that the wiring reaches my brain directly through my spine. And I can control a real robot, not one in virtual reality. You see, part of the long-term Mars Project was to use robots—which don't need oxygen, water, or heat—to explore Mars. However, the problem was that they couldn't think like humans.

And that's where I came in. When I was a baby, I had an experimental operation to insert a special rod with thousands of tiny, biological implant fibers into my spine. Each of the fibers has a core that transmits tiny impulses of electricity, allowing my brain to control a robot's computer. From all my years of training in a computer simulation program, my mind knows all the muscle moves it takes to handle the virtual-reality controls. Handling the robot is no different, except instead of actually moving my muscles, I imagine I'm moving the muscles. My brain sends the proper nerve impulses to the robot, and it moves the way I made the robot move in the virtual-reality computer program.

I admit, it's cool. Almost worth being in a wheelchair. For the operation had gone wrong, leaving me crippled.

Ashley was wired in the same way—with one difference. Because she'd had the operation on Earth, with better medical facilities, it didn't do any damage to her spine. She had the best of both worlds.

Other than that, we both could handle robots in the same way.

✳

"Still won't work," she said.

I raised an eyebrow. The way that Dad did. At least I thought it was the way Dad did.

Ashley giggled. "You need more practice."

"Huh?"

"With that eyebrow. I saw you the other day. Trying it in a mirror."

"Ant-bot," I said, hoping my face wasn't too red. "Why won't it work?"

"There's no gravity that would allow the ant-bot to crawl." Ashley pointed at a nearby handhold. "You and I are big enough to grab those and pull forward. But the ant-bot would just float around aimlessly. Even if we found a way to let it travel, how are you going to get into his bunker? You don't have the access code to his hatch door. It's not like last time, where your dad was using the mainframe computer to get us into all the different places on the ship."

"One step ahead of you," I said. "There's another way to get in. Through the air vent. Even without gravity on this ship, there's still air movement. That's why we have the vents. I'm saying we put the ant-bot in the right air vent and let the air blow it all the way down to his bunker. Then we leave it there to watch him later."

"Might work," she said. "Just might work."

"Of course it will. We could try it this afternoon and . . ."

I stopped as someone else floated into the exercise room.

Susan Fielding. In the regulation blue jumpsuit. She had a towel wrapped around her neck. As usual, she had an E-book with her.

"Hello," she said in her quiet voice. "Do you want me to come back later?"

"No," I said quickly. Dad had given Ashley and I permission to work on a feature article. This would be a great time to start learning more about the crew. "In fact, we were hoping to get the chance to spend some time with you. Ashley and I would like to interview you."

"Me?"

I nodded.

"I'm . . . I'm . . . not sure. Is this very important?"

I nodded again. More important than she could guess.

Unless, of course, she was the traitor. Then there was nothing for her to guess.

"I was born in Chicago," Susan Fielding said.

The three of us floated comfortably beside the weight equipment.

"Both my parents were scientists," she continued. "So it was only natural that I discovered the same kind of interest. I spent 10 years at a university, then another three in specialized training for the Mars Project."

I groaned. "Thirteen more years of school."

Ashley elbowed me. I bounced off her elbow and floated away. I had to find a handhold and use it to push myself back toward them.

"It's not that bad," Susan said, giving me a shy smile. "Not if you love the research and learning like I do."

"No kidding. I mean, genetics. Mom explained to me the basics. To think that scientists are able to engineer . . ."

I snapped my mouth shut so quickly that my teeth clacked. *Able to engineer different types of animals. And under the dome there had been an illegal attempt to . . .*

"You're thinking about the Martian koalas, aren't you?"

Susan Fielding said. Her pale cheeks began to flush. "I wasn't part of that project. And I was just as angry as anyone about the genetic manipulation of those animals. If you're going to use this article to accuse me of it, maybe we should stop this little interview right now."

"I'm not accusing you," I said. "I was just thinking about the koalas," I said. "How could I not? But—"

I was stuck.

"But the article will be much better if readers see how angry you were about it," Ashley said to her. "As a genetic scientist and as a person."

Susan relaxed.

Good save, Ashley, I thought. I also realized that I really *did* want to write this article. It would be interesting, getting the different opinions of people on the ship. It was too bad that a possible hidden bomb and an onboard traitor were the other reasons for writing it.

"So 13 years of work, just to get to Mars . . . ," Ashley prompted the scientist. "And a six-month trip across the middle of the solar system to get there. Do you think it was worth it?"

Susan nodded. "Every minute. Not just the science part. To be able to watch sunrises and sunsets on a different planet? To walk on the Martian sand and wonder about the universe? Incredible. And the bonus was that I got to work so hard on the genetic stuff too," she said, her voice growing louder and more enthusiastic.

"But you only stayed for one three-year shift," I said, almost without thinking. "Most scientists stay a lot longer after putting in all that effort to get there. And if you loved it so much, why leave?"

She shrank into herself, and her face became stone-cold. Grabbing her E-book, she tucked it under her arm.

"Obviously this is a real interview. Just like most of the media on Earth. Rude. I've had enough." Without saying good-bye, Susan Fielding yanked at a handhold. It threw her forward toward the hatch, and she barely ducked in time to make it through.

"Really know how to charm them, don't you?" Ashley said, hand on her hip in her traditionally annoyed pose.

I tried a weak grin. "You still like me, right?"

"Humph."

"Come on. She's hiding something. Why would she suddenly leave Mars?"

"Humph."

Obviously, Ashley didn't have an answer to that.

Which is what worried me the most.

CHAPTER 9

I floated into the computer control center. Aside from the navigation cone, it was the most important part of the ship. Dad explained it to me this way. If the *Moon Racer* was like a human body, the computer control center was the brain of the ship and the navigation cone, as it operated the movement of the ship, was the arms and legs that responded to the brain. With one slight difference. Since the pilot was the head commander in space, the navigational system—which depended on the computer control center—only worked after the pilot keyed in his password.

Other than this override from the navigational system, the computer control center monitored air, heating, communications, electrical, and all the dozens of other miniature systems that made life possible on the ship.

For such a crucial center, it didn't look like much.

There was a mainframe computer attached to the wall, with a monitor in front and another monitor to the side. On the opposite wall, a second and third computer, each with a monitor, served as emergency backups. A straight-backed chair faced the main computer. That was it. All was lit by the soft white glow of the recessed argon tubes.

Lance Evenson sat in front of the computer, his big shoulders blocking most of the screen.

He wasn't alone. Luke Daab, tool belt strapped to his waist, had a couple of computer wires in his hand. Beside the mainframe, he'd taken off some wall panels. The mess of different colored wires looked like a tangle of snakes. So close to Lance Evenson, Luke Daab looked even smaller and more shrunken than usual.

I coughed discreetly to let them both know I had entered the room.

Luke glanced at me, then away with his usual shyness.

Lance turned. And frowned at me. "What is it," he demanded. Not a question. But an almost angry statement.

"Um, Ashley and I are doing interviews for an article we want to write for people on Earth," I said. I didn't think Lance would agree to it, but I had to try. "We're wondering if you—"

"Not a chance," Lance snarled. "Trouble with too many people is that they don't mind their own business. Including you."

Lance shifted again and faced his computer monitor. Blips and lines danced with random movement on what little of the screen I could see past his massive body.

I coughed again.

"What is it," Lance said in his same angry tone, not bothering to look away from the computer.

I had two reasons for being here. One was to make sure Lance was in the computer room and wouldn't find Ashley and me at the air vent in the corridor near his bunker. And the other reason was just as important.

"I'm expecting an E-mail from Rawling," I said. "But it hasn't shown up on my comp-board."

"We're almost 40 million miles from Mars," Lance

Evenson growled, still watching the computer. "These things take time."

"I sent it late last night," I said. "I'm pretty sure he would have replied by now. Is there any chance it's somewhere on the mainframe?"

"Are you accusing me of keeping your private mail?"

"N-no . . . ," I stuttered. "Not at all. I'm just wondering—"

"That's another one of your problems," Lance said. "You wonder too much. I'll look into it. Now go away."

I grabbed a handhold and prepared to push off.

I noticed Luke Daab looking at me. Sadness seemed to fill his tiny, wrinkled face.

Then I realized something that made me feel guilty. I had totally ignored him. Like always. Like most people did, because he was a glorified janitor, almost invisible as he did the maintenance duties no one else wanted to do.

"Mr. Daab," I said, "would you be able to find time for an interview?"

"Yes," he said, suddenly smiling. "Thank you very much!"

In one way I felt better for asking him. And in another his eagerness made me feel even worse for first ignoring him.

"How about this afternoon?" I said, hiding my guilt.

"Great," he said.

"That's great with me," I said as I pushed away and floated out of the computer control center.

It *was* great.

By then Ashley and I would have had a chance to explore behind the vent in Lance Evenson's bunker. And maybe by then, we would have proved the chief computer technician was guilty of a lot more than just a bad temper.

CHAPTER 10

"Ready?" Ashley asked.

"Ready," I said.

"Checklist," she said.

On my back in the robot lab, I was strapped to the bed so that I couldn't move and accidentally break the connection between the antenna plug in my spine and the receiver across the room.

"One," I said, "no robot contact with any electrical sources."

My spinal nerves were attached to the plug. Any electrical current going into or through the robot would scramble the X-ray waves so badly that the signals reaching my brain would do serious damage.

"Two," I said, "I will disengage instantly at the first warning of any damage to the robot's computer drive."

My brain circuits worked so closely with the computer circuits that any harm to the computer would spill over to harm my brain.

"Last," I asked Ashley, "is the robot battery at full power?"

"Yes. And unplugged from the electrical source that charges it."

"I'm ready," I said.

"Let's go, then."

Ashley placed a soundproof headset on my ears. The fewer distractions to reach my brain in my real body, the better.

It was dark and silent while I waited for a sensation that had become familiar and beautiful for me. The sensation of entering the robot computer.

My wait did not take long. Soon I began to fall off a high, invisible cliff into a deep, invisible hole.

I kept falling and falling and falling. . . .

Halfway across the spaceship, tiny video lenses opened on the head of a robot smaller than an ant.

Those lenses translated light patterns into a digital code, which was beamed by X-ray waves into the computer that was attached to my body through the spinal wiring. The digital code retranslated in my own brain, just like light patterns that entered my own eyes. I saw what the ant-bot saw—a huge tunnel that looked about a mile across, striped with shadows from the light that came through the slits of the air-vent cover behind it.

The tunnel wasn't that wide, of course. But from the ant-bot's perspective, everything seemed monstrous. Except for the splinter of plastic from a broken DVD-gigarom cover in its left hand.

Earlier Ashley and I had found the vent cover at the closest entry point to the vent that led into Lance Evenson's bunker. We had taken the cover off and had attached the ant-bot—armed with its splinter of plastic—to the inside of the vent so that it wouldn't float away until we were ready.

Which was now.

In my own mind I gave a command for the ant-bot's right hand to let go of the inside of the vent cover. Immediately the flow of air spun the ant-bot farther into the vent.

Without the force of gravity, the ant-bot bounced and danced along the river of moving air like a speck of dust. I brought the right hand over to grip the splinter of plastic. I held the tiny spear of plastic crossways in front of me. And waited for the air to take me to my destination.

The light that had reached the inside of the vent through the cover fell behind me, and darkness overwhelmed the ant-bot.

It was an eerie sensation of nothingness. No light. No sound. No gravity. And because I saw and heard nothing through the robot's video or audio, there was nothing to indicate that I was still moving. For all I could tell, I would be held by this darkness forever. I told myself otherwise, of course, and waited as patiently as I could.

With nothing to help my senses understand my surroundings, time stretched far too slowly. I was almost ready to believe that I was stuck forever in the darkness when the first dim light reached the ant-bot's video lenses. It came from Lance's bunker.

With the new stripes of that light growing brighter, I tried to orient the ant-bot so it faced the vent directly. It was impossible. The air tumbled the ant-bot in unpredictable directions.

The air-vent cover loomed larger and larger so that it looked like the face of a giant cliff as the ant-bot swept into it.

The slits of the cover were so big that the ant-bot could

be sucked through it with the passing air. That's why I held the splinter of plastic. Like a crossbeam, the plastic slammed into the vent and held the ant-bot in place.

Slowly I released the ant-bot's right hand from the plastic and gripped the edge of the nearest vent cover slit. Once it was firmly attached, I was able to direct one of the video lenses to look back in the direction I had just traveled.

It took a couple of seconds to make sense of what I saw in the striped shadows of the air vent slits. Especially because everything seemed so gigantic from the view of the ant-bot.

But then I realized what Lance was hiding. It wasn't in his bunker. It was here in the air vent.

A DVD-gigarom disc. Taped to the surface of the vent.

CHAPTER 11

"Where were you born?" I asked Luke Daab. "How big was your family? When did you start dreaming of going to Mars?"

We were the only two in the entertainment cluster. A giant screen filled one wall. The ship had hundreds of movies in DVD-gigarom format. Six months was a long time to travel, and the 3-D movies really helped ease the boredom.

"Slow down, slow down," he said with a shy smile. "I can't think that fast."

"Where were you born?" It was a good thing I had a list of prepared questions. My heart was not really in this interview. I was worried about what might happen to the ant-bot. And more worried about what Lance had hidden behind the vent in his bunker area. I was only here because I had agreed to meet Luke at this time and because Dad was too busy to see me right now.

"Key West," Luke said. He scratched his wrinkly, little face. "It's at the southern tip of Florida."

"Near Cuba," I added, thinking of my geography lessons.

"Near Cuba," he confirmed. "But remember, when I

grew up, Cuba still wasn't one of the states of America. And shortly after it joined, the United States led the way for a world-federated government. Things have really changed since I was your age."

"Sounds like you miss it," I said without thinking. I had my list of questions to go through, and I should have stuck with it so that this interview would end as quickly as possible. I had lots to do—as soon as Dad was finished with his computer check. Strange glitches had been showing up, and they were driving him crazy.

"When I was a kid," Luke said, his face twisting, "we had freedom. I could fish when and where I wanted. Sail across the water without a satellite camera filming me. My family could go on vacation without reporting it to the government first. There were no microchips to track everything a person did."

"From what I understand," I said cautiously, "people haven't lost much freedom and for that small loss of freedom have gained a lot of security. They—"

"You don't know what it was like! You haven't spent any time on Earth, but you still buy the arguments about a controlled economy and lack of crime!"

My eyes must have opened wide in surprise at his outburst. It seemed so unlike the Luke I'd seen quietly move about the spaceship for the past five-plus months.

"Sorry," he said, the shy smile back in place. "That probably answers another one of your questions. Why I wanted to go to Mars. I thought a planet with no people on it might be a place of freedom."

"And . . ."

"You can call me a maintenance engineer in your article," he smiled sadly, "but no matter what job title I get, I'm still a janitor. And janitors don't get treated much differently on Mars than they do on Earth. I didn't get much of a chance to see the planet."

"Oh."

"Don't get me wrong. It was still worth it. I was there when the dome was built, and this is my first trip back to Earth. If I hadn't liked it, I would have applied to come back much earlier."

"I guess 15 years on Mars was long enough. . . ." This was leading me to the one question Ashley and I wanted everyone to answer: Why they were going back to Earth. What reason they had for being on this ship with Blaine Steven and Dr. Jordan. If it seemed like they didn't have a good reason, it might be the first hint that something wasn't right.

"Maybe not," Luke answered. "But my father is really, really ill. I decided if I didn't go back now, I wouldn't have a chance to help my mother. As you can imagine, they are both very old."

I scanned the rest of my questions. There were four left, but I was itching to get to Dad and tell him what I knew. Luke had already answered the most important question about his reason for leaving Mars.

"Thanks, Mr. Daab," I said. "That really helps."

"That's it?"

I nodded. "That's it."

"Just as well," he said. "I have lots to do."

The sad part was that I think he knew I just wanted to get out of there. And even sadder, I think he expected it because he was just a janitor.

I tried not to think about it anymore as I looked for Dad to tell him my news.

CHAPTER 12

"Let me get this straight," Dad said sternly. "You made an unauthorized use of the ant-bot and invaded the privacy of one of the members of the ship? And then you left the ant-bot—worth only about two billion dollars of technological research—attached to the inside of the air-vent cover in his bunker?"

I squirmed. A person wouldn't think that weightlessness would ever be uncomfortable but, even floating in midair, I couldn't find a position that felt right.

"I thought that if I found something that—"

"That the results would justify whatever way you did it?"

By the coldness in Dad's voice, I knew I was wrong to think *yes*. Even more, I was wrong to not consult him, as pilot, first. "We didn't invade his privacy," I said quietly, trying to find a way to defend myself. "We didn't spy on him. We just went into the place where you had wanted me to vacuum earlier to search for the same thing. Remember? You asked us to look for whatever might be behind the vent covers in any of the bunkers."

Dad sat on his pilot's chair. He had swiveled it away from the controls of the navigation cone as I'd entered. The black, star-studded sky, visible through the clear shell of the navigation cone, framed his broad shoulders. His eyes bored into mine.

"Earlier, you were doing it under the pilot's express directions. Now without the pilot's authorization, you have, by government law and by military ship regulations, engaged in a criminal act of utmost seriousness." The coldness did not leave his voice. "Furthermore, now that I have knowledge of your crime, I must take action against you. If not, again by government law and by military ship regulations, I too am guilty of this serious crime. Regardless of your intentions, any court-martial assembly would have no choice but to strip me of my pilot's license and possibly sentence me to jail time."

I closed my eyes as all of this sunk in. To me, it had been a good solution to helping Dad solve the ship's crisis—without getting anyone else involved. I'd never dreamed I'd cause so much trouble.

"Now let me speak to you as a father, not the pilot," Dad said with a sigh. I opened my eyes as the coldness left his voice. He put a hand on my shoulder. "Tyce," he said gently, "you've placed me in a very difficult position. I'm not afraid to risk my career as a pilot. You're far more important to me than that. But to protect you, I would have to break my oath as a pilot. I would have to live a lie and, as a Christian, I can't live that way. . . ."

He let his voice trail into silence as he looked away from me. "Yet to do what the law and my oath require of me will hurt you more than I can bear."

I could think of no reply.

"Tell me," he said, still staring off into the emptiness of the solar system, "did you find something that threatens the safety of the ship and passengers? Some sort of explosive? Anything like that?"

"No," I said. "But—"

"Stop there!"

I did.

"I don't want to hear what you found."

"But—"

A long, long silence followed before he began again. "Tyce, by the pilot's code, the safety of ship and passengers takes priority over any other matter. I could make a case in military court for protecting you and acting on your information if we faced a threat. Otherwise . . ."

Again he sighed. He turned and faced me. "I have no choice." Dad picked up a cordless microphone from the console of the controls. Putting it to his mouth, he pushed a button on the side of it. He spoke quietly, entering the date and time into the audio-log of the computer.

"Captain's report," he continued. "This is a formal report of a privacy violation enacted by passenger Tyce Sanders against chief computer technician Lance Evenson. As this is a first-time offense by said passenger, he is placed on a two-week probationary period. He is also instructed to make a formal apology to Lance Evenson within the next 24 hours."

Twenty-four hours? That was strange. If it was as serious as Dad said, why wouldn't he make me apologize immediately?

Dad clicked off the microphone and set it aside.

"I'm sorry, Dad," I said, hanging my head.

"Me too," he said. "The worst of it is that it sounds like I should know what you found."

"Yes, sir."

"But as it stands right now, if you told me, I would not be

able to act upon illegally obtained information. I can only act if there is danger to the ship and passengers, or unless it was obtained by direct orders from the pilot."

"Yes, sir."

"Tyce, the rules and regulations of space travel have been set up to safeguard passengers. But rules and regulations are black-and-white. They can never be perfect and can never anticipate every situation. Nor can they perfectly deal with gray situations like this."

"Yes, sir."

"You understand that since you are on probation, if you violate any other rules of space travel, I must lock you in your bunker for the duration of the trip."

"Yes, sir."

"Having said that, I now give you a direct order to do your best to deliver me information that has been found in such a way that no court could dispute the legality with which it has been obtained."

"Sir?"

He looked at his watch, then smiled at me. "The clock is ticking, son. In 23 hours and 56 minutes, by direct and recorded orders from the pilot of this ship, you are going to have to explain to Lance Evenson what you did and apologize for your actions."

"Sir?"

"Much as I didn't want to, I first had to address what you did by strictly following regulations, especially if any of this comes to trial. But my first priority as captain is to get this ship to Earth, and I will now move past the regulations, which don't cover a situation like this. What I'm telling you is that you now have 23 hours, 55 minutes, and 35 seconds to undo your mistake and find a way to get me the information you feel is vital to the continued operation of this ship. When we arrive on Earth, I will report everything. Including my instructions to you. If my handling of this situation is wrong, I intend to share whatever punishment you might receive."

CHAPTER 13

From: "Rawling McTigre" <mctigrer@marsdome.ss>
To: Tyce Sanders <sanderst@marsdome.ss>
Sent: 03.06.2040, 11:39 A.M.
Subject: Re: questions

Tyce,
Sorry I don't have anything to tell you at this point. If I learn anything that will be helpful, I'll let you know as soon as possible. Rawling

I stared at my comp-board screen and reread the message three times. I'd finally received the E-mail from Rawling, but I had hoped for a lot more. *Where's the background information on the passengers? Doesn't Rawling understand it's important enough that we need it, no matter how busy he is?*

I read it again, as if that would help. Which it didn't.

Is Rawling mad at me? Normally, he ended all his E-mails to me by signing off with *"carpe diem,* Rawls." He'd once told me that *carpe diem* was Latin for "seize the day." It was the motto he tried to live by. He said that it was important to live bravely, and he hoped I would always remember that.

Why hadn't he reminded me to seize the day, like he did in all his other E-mails to me? I also noticed the time the E-mail had been sent. An hour after I had asked Lance about it. Which was 12 hours after I'd sent the first E-mail to Rawling.

Weird. I expected that Rawling would have replied much quicker.

I thought about it awhile, then hit the reply button to his E-mail and began to keyboard a message in return.

From: "Tyce Sanders" <sanderst@marsdome.ss>
To: Rawling McTigre <mctigrer@marsdome.ss>
Sent: 03.06.2040, 2:51 P.M.
Subject: Re: questions

Rawling,

Thanks for getting back to me. I know you are doing your best. I think we have a little time before it absolutely becomes crucial. In the meantime, take care of your sore elbow. Remember, you're not the young hockey player anymore that I've heard so much about during your university days. Tyce

I hit the send button and smiled grimly. His reply to this message would tell me a lot of what I needed to know.

And in the meantime, I had other questions to ask of someone else.

I opened up a word processsing file on my comp-board and let my fingers fly across the keyboard.

Even as I concentrated on the words popping up on the screen, I was too aware of how little time I had left before my next appointment.

❋

"Hello," I said to the man hooked to the wall by cable. I had tucked my comp-board under my arm. "Yesterday, you said you wanted to talk. So I'm here."

"Good," Steven replied. "Let's talk about God. You'd be surprised at how interested I am."

He was right. I would be surprised—if he really meant it. Frankly, after all the things Steven had done, I'd written him off a long time ago. Mom always talked about God being so big that no one was ever beyond his reach, but sometimes it was hard for me to believe that. Especially around people like Blaine Steven and Dr. Jordan.

Somehow I still assumed that his faith question had been an excuse to talk for the benefit of whoever might be listening in on our conversation.

"Tell me," he said, "if something happened to the *Moon Racer* and I died in the next two weeks, why would God ever want anything to do with me? I mean, I haven't exactly been the best person in the world."

I laughed. "Neither have I."

He looked surprised. "You haven't tried to kill anyone or take over the Mars Dome or . . ."

I repeated how Mom had explained it to me: "If a person had to jump from Earth to the moon, would it make any difference if he could jump six inches off the ground or six feet? Either way, he doesn't have a chance."

"True, but what does this have to do with my question?"

"Nobody can make himself perfect enough to get to God," I said. "No matter what you've done compared to what I have or haven't done, neither of us can jump to the moon."

"And?"

"It's the same with God. We can't get to him by ourselves. We need his help. But he's waiting for us—to reach for him. Then he forgives us and gives us love, instead of what we really deserve."

I could see Steven was listening. I was really glad that Mom and I had had talks about this.

"I know my mom and dad love me," I continued. "But if I decided I wanted to have nothing to do with them for the rest of my life, no amount of their love could make me return to them. All they could do was wait for me to want them in my life again. And as soon as I reached out to them, they would welcome me back with open arms."

"And you're saying it's the same with God?" Steven said, looking intrigued.

"If you pretend he doesn't exist—just like if I pretended my parents don't exist—how can he ever be part of your life? Or you part of him?"

Steven looked puzzled. "That gives me a lot to think about." He let out a deep breath and pointed at my comp-board.

Wordlessly I opened up my comp-board and fired up the word processing program. When the screen showed my questions, I carefully reached across the space between us and handed it to him.

He scanned the screen and nodded.

"Good-bye," I said. "I'll probably be back in an hour. If you'd like to talk some more."

"That would be fine," Steven said. He didn't lift his head. He had already begun to type.

CHAPTER 14

Every time I tried to move quickly from handhold to handhold, I thought of the old movie about Tarzan of the jungle, swinging through the vines. I resisted the urge to make a jungle noise as I sped toward the simulation center, exactly halfway across the ship. Ashley was waiting for me, and I had an idea I wanted to share with her.

As I followed the curve of the corridor's circle, the light seemed dimmer. Seconds later I saw why as I almost hit Luke Daab. He was hanging in midair in the center of the corridor, with a lighting panel floating beside him. One argon tube hung beside the panel. He had another tube in his hand and was replacing the first one. A few scattered tools hung in the air nearby.

"Hey, Mr. Daab," I said. As I pushed quickly to one side I had a glimpse of all the wiring in the corridor's ceiling. I narrowly missed him and his tools as I aimed for the corridor wall directly beside him. When I hit the wall, I pushed off again toward the center. It put me right back at the handholds on the opposite side of him. I reached for the next handhold and kept going. I called over my shoulder. "See you later!"

"Good-bye, Tyce," he said. "Be careful!"

Careful? From my wheelchair all my life I had watched people walk or run past me on strong, healthy legs. To me this was the closest I would ever get to any kind of real freedom outside of my wheelchair. It was too much fun for me to worry about being careful.

A much darker thought hit me as I continued to swing from handhold to handhold.

If the spaceship never made it to Earth, how much would it matter if I was careful or not?

"What's that?" Ashley asked once I reached our computer station. She had her own comp-board in front of her, screen flipped open.

"Regulation jumpsuit," I said. I had folded the blue jumpsuit across my right arm. "Picked it up on the way here." I decided I wouldn't tell Ashley about my run-in with Dad; she and I had enough other things to think about.

"I know it's a jumpsuit. *Why* do you have it?"

"If you wanted to know why, you should have asked that in the first place."

"Tyce!" She flashed her dark eyes at me.

"Ashley!" I said, imitating her.

She sighed and shook her head. "I guess I'll be the mature one and move right along to the serious business and tell you about the rest of the interviews."

"Sure," I said, still grinning. I was in a great mood. And she would find out why very soon.

"I managed to speak to everyone else," she said. "As it turns out I didn't discover anything unusual. But I know why Susan Fielding is going back to Earth so soon."

"Oh?" With my right hand, I grabbed the sleeve of the

jumpsuit near the shoulder. With my left hand, I held the rest of the jumpsuit.

"She needs some medical checkups. I couldn't find out exactly what kind, but that's what Jack Tripp was able to tell me when I interviewed him. And I can tell you there doesn't seem to be anything strange in what he told me about himself. What do you think we should do next, since—"

I yanked as hard as I could. With a loud rip, the sleeve began to separate from the rest of the jumpsuit.

"What are you doing?" Ashley asked.

"Ripping off a sleeve."

"I can see that. But *why* are you—"

"If you wanted to know why, you should have asked that in the first place."

"Aaaaaarghh."

I grinned again. Yes, I was in a good mood. I knew exactly how we were going to prove Lance Evenson was behind this.

I plucked at the loosened material in my hands.

"Ashley," I said, "when I'm finished with this, you'll be ready to call me a genius."

I explained as I continued to unravel threads from the jumpsuit.

And she, too, began to smile.

CHAPTER 15

Half an hour later, Ashley and I returned to the robot lab. Much as I wanted to rush through the checklist process, Ashley forced us to go slowly.

Finally, I was strapped in place, in darkness and silence.

Then, as always, came the sensation of falling . . . falling . . .

My return to sight brought the striped shadows of the air-vent cover of Lance Evenson's bunker. Those shadows fell on the DVD-gigarom disc that was taped to the inside of the vent.

I brought one of the ant-bot arms up in front of me. I waggled it, simply because I never got tired of working a robot through the nerve impulses sent by my brain. Incredible as the ant-bot's engineering might be, I didn't intend to try to move the disc or carry it.

No, even here in the weightlessness of outer space, that would take something else.

I didn't have to wait long.

Just as the air current had earlier sent the ant-bot floating down here to the vent cover, it now brought something else.

Thread.

Or, more precisely, one thread tied to another thread tied to another and another and another.

I had taken threads from the jumpsuit and knotted them to form a long, long single thread. Then, to make sure the air current would bring the thread down the vent, I had tied one end to a small square of paper.

Through the video lens of the ant-bot, I watched that small square approach, like a sail ahead of a breeze in one of the pirate movies I loved to watch. The thread trailing behind it was invisible in the darkness of the vent shaft. But when the paper reached the vent cover, I was easily able to grab the piece of thread in the tiny robot hand. I pulled it loose from the piece of paper.

The only tricky part would come next.

Because of the lack of gravity, I could not simply let go of the vent cover and expect to drop. I would have to launch the ant-bot in the direction of the disc.

Seconds later I made the leap.

Although I only covered about six inches, to the ant-bot it was like a jump that covered five football fields.

As the ant-bot floated through the air, I tied one end of the thread around the ant-bot's other arm. Although it was just a thread of fabric, it seemed like a rope. When I landed, I had the rope securely lashed. Then both of the ant-bot's arms were free for use.

There wasn't much surface on the disc small enough for the ant-bot to actually get a grip on it. But it didn't matter.

I had timed my jump well enough to land beside the single strand of tape that held the disc against the inside surface of the vent.

First I pried a small part of the edge of the tape off the disc. I unwrapped the thread from the ant-bot arm and pushed it against the sticky underside of the tape. I tugged. It wasn't much of a tug. A human hand would have easily ripped the thread loose. But the ant-bot didn't have that kind of strength, and the thread remained in place.

Then I began the longer task of cutting the tape where it joined between the disc and the vent.

The ant-bot hands were tiny, and the tape seemed as thick as a slice of bread might look to human eyes. But since ant-bot hands were made of titanium, it was easy to claw through the tape.

When I finished cutting the tape on both sides of the disc, I had one last little task.

I pulled on the thread to get a little slack. I looped it a couple of times around the ant-bot's neck. Then in my mind I shouted "Stop!" Instantly I woke up back in the computer room.

Ashley and I stood in the corridor with a vent cover hanging beside us.

She held a piece of thread in her hands and slowly pulled.

Because there was no gravity, I knew she didn't feel the weight of the disc on the other end of the thread. But she kept pulling, trusting that the ant-bot had done the job properly.

As she kept reeling in thread, the disc appeared. She grabbed it with her hand and gave it to me.

I loosened the thread where the ant-bot had stuck it to

CHAPTER 16

"This is it, Ashley." I waved my opened comp-board at her. "In five minutes, we're going to have all the answers."

We were back in the entertainment cluster, alone. It had taken hardly any time at all to retrieve my comp-board from Blaine Steven.

"How can you know that? You haven't even opened the disc yet."

"I'm not talking just the disc." It was in the front pocket of my jumpsuit. All I needed to do was fit it into the discport on the right-hand side of the comp-board, and we'd find out what was on it. But first the other information. "Blaine Steven had my comp-board for the last hour. He—"

"Blaine Steven? You let him access your computer?"

I explained why. "See this," I said, as I clicked on the file with my questions for him. The words sprang into shape on my screen. I leaned over to let Ashley share my view of it. "I put in the questions and he's given the answers."

I read it silently with her.

> Why do you think Dr. Jordan and this mastermind person want you dead?

Because I know how the Terratakers work. I know too much about them. I can expose them and testify against them. They don't care whether I ever intend to do anything against them. They will get rid of me simply because it is a safe thing to do. I was never afraid of them when I was on Mars, because they needed me when I was director. But as I get closer to Earth, I am more afraid. Especially because I hear Dr. Jordan having conversations in the bunker beside me. I can't hear the words; I just know that someone is visiting him late at night. The mastermind. I know that if they wanted me to continue to be part of the rebels, the mastermind would come to my bunker too. But they are leaving me alone.

Why would they want everyone else on the ship dead?

Because it is safe for them. If they escape the *Moon Racer*, they will be picked up by a rebel space shuttle. Dr. Jordan won't be arrested then. The mastermind will be able to disappear into the underworld of the Terratakers, who are spread all across the world. And if they are the only survivors, no one will ever be able to talk about them.

Why should I believe anything you tell me?

If you don't believe me now, you will when something starts going wrong with the *Moon Racer*. If it isn't an explosive device, which is my first guess, it will be something else. I hope I'm wrong about all of this. If we make it to Earth

safely, then you can laugh at me as the military
officials arrest me.

Why should Dad or I help you?
    I have many, many secrets that can help the
World United defeat the rebels before they find a
way to start a new world war. That is their goal.
Once a war begins and the confederation of countries splits up, they can take advantage of the
confusion and of the weaker countries.

I was about to comment when, *Bing!* The tiny noise from
my comp-board jolted me away from the words on the
screen.
    My E-mail announcement. Mail had just arrived.
    "Hang on," I said to Ashley. I clicked a few buttons on
the keyboard to open my E-mail. "Hopefully it's from
Rawling. That will give us even more information."
    The E-mail symbol jumped into the foreground of the
screen, leaving my question-and-answer interview with
Blaine Steven in the background.
    I double-clicked to open the new E-mail.
    "Yup," I said. "Rawling."

From: "Rawling McTigre" <mctigrer@marsdome.ss>
To: Tyce Sanders <sanderst@marsdome.ss>
Sent: 03.06.2040 4:13 P.M.
Subject: Re: questions

Tyce,
    *I still don't have anything to tell you that might be of help. I'll
keep looking, however, and get to you immediately if I learn
anything. Rawling*

P.S. The elbow is getting better. I know it hurts me a lot less than it hurt other people in my old hockey days on Earth!

"I knew it!" I said. I pointed at the screen. "I just knew it!"

"Tyce, if you get any more excited, you'll start to drool." Ashley frowned. "And I don't see much to get excited about."

"He normally signs off differently." I told Ashley about the Latin phrase that meant "seize the day" and how Rawling always ended his E-mails to me with *"carpe diem, Rawls."*

"So he forgot," Ashley said. "He *is* director of the Mars Dome. Plus, he's got to be worried about this spaceship. With everything else happening on Mars . . ."

"He's also taking a lot longer than usual to reply."

"Because he's taking all that time to try to find answers for you."

I shook my head. "The Rawling I know would fire off an immediate E-mail explaining that it might take awhile to get what he needs."

"The Rawling you know? Meaning this Rawling is—"

"Someone else." I pointed at the P.S. of the E-mail and read it out loud. " 'The elbow is getting better. I know it hurts me a lot less than it hurt other people in my old hockey days on Earth!' "

"Even I understand what he means," Ashley said, still unimpressed at my excitement. "In hockey, players some-times elbow other players."

"Not Rawling. He didn't play hockey in his university days. He played football."

Ashley's eyes widened as she began to understand.

"Look at my original E-mail to him."

She reread it with me. *Remember, you're not the young hockey player anymore that I've heard so much about during your university days. Tyce.*

"I wrote that because I knew he was a quarterback. If it was Rawling who received the message and if it was Rawling who wrote back, he would have corrected me, not agreed with me!"

"Someone else is intercepting your E-mail?"

"And who has control of the computers on board this ship?"

"Lance Evenson!" Ashley was getting as excited as I was. "The same guy who hid a disc."

"Yes," I said. "The same guy who—"

I hit my head. "No, no, no!" I began to fumble with my comp-board.

"Tyce?" Ashley asked.

I didn't take the time to answer. I frantically clawed at a small compartment on the underside of my keyboard. I needed to pull out the battery and shut down my computer.

In front of our eyes, the words on the comp-board screen were beginning to dissolve.

The same person who had intercepted my E-mail was logged on to my computer through the mainframe. And trying to destroy all the information on it!

CHAPTER 17

"Dad!" I shouted. "Dad!"

I wasn't even all the way down the tube that led to the navigation cone. "Dad! Are you there!"

If he wasn't in front of his controls, I didn't want to waste time going all the way down and then back up.

"Yes, I'm here, Tyce." His calm voice helped me relax. He would know what to do. And how to do it.

I dropped into the navigation cone. Dad spun around in his chair. His face was tired.

"I think I have the answers you need," I said.

"Good, because I don't seem to be getting anywhere by myself. What have you got?"

"A quick quiz."

"Ready."

"What," I asked, "do all of these have in common: ship controls, escape pod controls, E-mail, networks, and Lance Evenson?"

I answered it for him. "Mainframe computer. All of the commands you give through the controls here are handled by the mainframe. Right? Same with everything else. In fact, just about every single thing on this ship is controlled through the mainframe. And who handles the mainframe? Lance Evenson."

"He doesn't have all the passwords. Without them, he can't override the pilot controls."

"Say somehow he did. Then won't you agree he's the one person who would have complete control of the ship? The one person who could activate an escape pod as soon as he needs it?"

"Well . . ."

"Follow me," I said. "And hopefully I can prove it."

He rose from his pilot's chair.

"Dad?"

"Yes, Tyce."

"You'd better unlock your neuron gun for this."

We met Ashley back at the entertainment cluster. She had her own comp-board open on her lap.

"Did it work?" I asked her.

She nodded. "I plugged the ethernet port on the back of the comp-board by pressing my finger against it, just like you suggested."

"Good," I said. With my comp-board out of commission, Ashley had gone to get hers while I found Dad. "And did you find what I thought you'd find on Lance's disc?"

Ashley nodded again. "A security override program. If I'm reading it correctly, it looks like I can get anywhere inside the mainframe with it."

"Dad?" I said softly.

"This is serious. But it still doesn't explain how someone on the mainframe can interfere with the pilot controls. My password is only registered on Earth, with the military, and it's under the tightest security you could imagine. It would only be given out in an emergency situation, if some-one else had to take over this ship."

"There's more on this disc," Ashley said. She held out the comp-board screen.

Dad looked over my shoulder. When he saw the con-tents of the disc, he whistled. "Look at the labels on those files! Communication files. E-mail files. Reports and docu-ments. It's like years of information stolen from the Mars Dome computer!"

"How much would that be worth on Earth?" I asked. "All that information? Sold to the wrong people like the rebels?"

Dad shook his head. "Enough, I guess, that whoever owned this disc would find it worthwhile to let everyone else on the ship die. I just never thought it would be Lance."

Dad made his decision. "What we do next is take this disc to Lance. We'll see what he has to say about it."

Ashley and I followed.

I couldn't help but notice that as Dad led the way, he touched the neuron gun on his hip. As if he were making sure it was there and ready.

CHAPTER 18

"No," Lance said. He groaned. "That's my disc. But it's not me doing everything else."

Dad and I and Ashley had met him at the computer control center. Dad had not said much beyond a quiet hello before asking permission to insert the disc into the mainframe.

When the contents of the disc had appeared on the monitor in front of Lance, he'd covered his face with his hands.

To me, it was the action of a guilty man. I found it difficult to keep my mouth shut. But Dad was the pilot. Dad would handle this.

"You don't sound surprised to find out someone has been using the mainframe for all of this," Dad said. "You're saying someone else has?"

"I have nothing more to say." Lance folded his big arms across his big chest. "Except that I have done nothing to threaten the safety of this ship."

"Prove it then," Dad said, still quiet. "Open the log of your mainframe computer activities."

"All right," Lance said after several seconds of thought.

He began to punch out a series of commands on his keyboard. "You'll see I'm innocent of that."

"But guilty of something else? Like possession of a master disc with a security override program? And with masses of highly confidential Mars Dome files?"

"I have nothing more to say in that regard. But I did nothing to threaten the safety of this ship. And if you look at the activity log . . ." Lance gasped. Lines of numbers showed brightly on the screen. "Impossible," he said. "Totally impossible. I look at this log at least three times a day and I've never seen these numbers before."

"What?" Dad asked.

Lance touched his index finger to the screen and followed a line of numbers. "Here. A command to unlock the prisoner's cable in bunker number five, just past midnight last night. Then to open the hatch to the corridor. And a command to seal it again two hours later. I . . . I . . . did not program this."

Bunker number five? That's Dr. Jordan's bunker. He's been out of his prison bunker for two hours?

"Let me get this straight," Dad said. "Someone released Jordan last night. And then Jordan returned to the prison bunker."

So Blaine Steven has not been lying about a mastermind on board!

Lance scanned the lines. "And the night before. And the night before that. In fact, it looks like Jordan has come and gone at his convenience almost since the ship left Mars."

"Why would you do that?" Dad asked.

"It wasn't me. I can tell you that. The man gives me the creeps."

"You want me to believe that someone else on this ship actually controls the mainframe." Dad's voice grew louder.

Lance ignored him and continued to scan the lines of the computer activity log. "Here. Unauthorized log-on to a personal comp-board. ID code 0808."

ID code 0808. My comp-board!

"What time?" I asked.

"More than once," Lance told me, reading the lines of code. "Including less than a half hour ago. Whoever logged on stole all the information on it and kept updating all the new information you added."

That person then knew about the secret conversations I was having with Blaine Steven!

"And here," Lance said, unaware of my anger and fear. "Disable commands to the escape pods. And here, commands that override the pilot controls."

That explained the malfunctions Dad had been fighting.

Lance looked at Dad with bewilderment. He had the face of a big kid, scared. "Wasn't me. I didn't do any of this!"

"Then who?"

"If I knew, I would tell you," Lance answered. "It could be anyone on this ship with a comp-board and the right security codes to access the mainframe."

"How? You don't let anyone into this computer room, do you?"

"I don't know how," Lance said in frustration.

"Think!" Dad said. "How would you do it?"

Lance shrugged his big shoulders. "I'd tap into a wire off the back of the mainframe and run that wire out somewhere in the ship. But not to my bunker, because it would be too easy to get caught. Instead, I'd run it to an infrared antenna that could be hidden anywhere and link from my comp-board that way. But you can't run that wire from this mainframe without time and access. Nobody has had either in this computer room."

He caught Dad's glare. "I know! I know! Then it really looks like I'm the one. But I'm not."

"I can order a search of all the comp-boards on the ship," Dad said. "That will prove you right. Or wrong. In the meantime, undo all those commands. Get the escape pods in working condition. Most of all, give me complete control again of the navigation cone."

"If I can," Lance said. He had his finger on the screen, running it below one of the lines.

"If you can?"

"This code . . . I have to figure out the code before I can override it."

"Which means?"

"Whoever has been tapping into the mainframe has complete control. Without the computer that's been instructing the mainframe, it will be impossible to undo all the commands that came from it."

"Then we'll begin looking," Dad said grimly. "In the meantime, I expect total cooperation from you."

Dad stared at Lance. Lance stared right back at him.

I looked beyond them at the computer screen.

"Dad?" I said. "Dad!"

The numbers on the screen began to dissolve. At the same time, the hatch door to the computer room began to close.

CHAPTER 19

Dad reacted first. He shoved off a handhold and made a midair dive for the hatch door. It shut squarely on his body, pinning him in the opening, with his legs inside the computer room and his upper body stuck in the corridor.

Normally a hatch door was sequenced by the computer to reopen if it hit any objects. This was a built-in safety feature to prevent exactly what had just happened.

I pushed toward him. "Dad? You all right?"

"Not good," Dad grunted from the other side. The hatch door pressed hard against his ribs. "Tyce, find something to jam in here so I can squeeze out. I don't know what's happening, but the last thing I want is us trapped in this room. Or unable to reenter once we are outside."

I looked behind me. There was nothing I could use. Just the mainframe computer, the monitor, a desk, and the chair Lance Evenson was strapped on. The rest was bare walls and ceiling.

"Hurry, Tyce," Dad grunted. "I think the door has got my diaphragm. I can't breathe!"

Being trapped or not suddenly seemed a lot less important than saving Dad's life. I rushed back to the hatch. I wedged one hand against the edge of the open hatchway and the other against the partly closed door. I tried to pull them apart. I pulled so hard that my vision turned black and I saw little stars.

"I . . . can't!"

I peered back at Lance Evenson, who was staring at me from his desk in front of the computer monitor.

"Please . . . I need help!"

This was the moment. If Lance was really the mastermind and had lied when he told us it was someone else controlling the ship's computer, then he'd let my dad die.

I futilely tried to pull again. "Help!"

It seemed like he moved in slow motion, but finally Lance came toward me, with Ashley following.

Lance took over my position. This was the first time I was glad that he was such a big man.

I backed up and inspiration hit me.

The ceiling panels!

I reached up and grabbed a handhold with my left hand. With my right, I yanked at a ceiling panel. It came loose. It was a square piece of plastic, about a foot wide and an inch thick. I didn't know if one would do it. I yanked another loose. Then a third.

I spun back toward the hatch. With all three tiles stacked together, I put the bottom into the opening first, beneath Dad's legs. The opening was less than a foot wide, however, and I could not wedge the top of the square into place.

Below where Dad was stuck in the hatch, Lance was straining hard, veins bulging in his neck as he struggled to slide open the hatch door. Above Dad, Ashley had braced herself by jamming her feet against the edge of the hatchway and pulling on the hatch with both hands. She was bent like a bow and screaming with effort.

Slowly the hatch door moved back. As Dad slipped out, I jammed the ceiling tiles in place.

Lance and Ashley let go of the hatch, and it slammed against the wedged tiles.

Dad pushed backward and let out a deep breath. "Good," he said, as the tiles held in place. "Now we're not trapped."

I let out my own sigh of relief.

Just then the spaceship jolted forward with sudden acceleration. All of us were hurled against the back wall.

"Is someone at the controls?" Dad shouted at Lance.

They both shoved themselves back toward the computer monitor.

Seconds later Lance gave us the answer we didn't want to hear. "Negative. Nobody is in the navigation cone," he answered as he read the monitor. "It looks like the computer has somehow been preprogrammed to do this. And the acceleration is continuing!"

As he finished speaking, the wailing sound of an alarm siren filled the ship.

My eyes met Dad's. We both knew that there was only one reason for that sound.

Someone had just begun the escape pod countdown.

CHAPTER 20

The corridor was strangely empty.

The siren wailed its piercing shriek to give notice that time was running out before the escape pod ejected. In the past few months, Dad had run the occasional drill—even during the night a couple of times—to prepare all of us for an emergency situation. Once the siren sounded there was less than three minutes to reach the pod.

But none of the ship's passengers had left their bunkers to see what was happening.

Just as well.

We swung from handhold to handhold, moving as fast as we could down the corridor toward the escape pods. If the others had wandered out of their bunkers into our path, it would have made for a disastrous collision.

The walls of the corridor seemed to blur in the confusion of our frantic scuttling. The noise gained in volume.

And finally we rounded the curve to reach the escape pods.

Just in time to see Dr. Jordan with Luke Daab.

They saw the three of us.

Luke's mouth moved, like he was shouting for us. But his words were drowned out by the siren.

"Stop!" Dad yelled uselessly above the din of the siren. I could barely hear him myself, and I was right beside his shoulder. "Stop!" He pulled his neuron gun from his belt and aimed. "Stop!" he shouted again.

Dr. Jordan might not have been able to hear Dad, but he could see the gun. We were less than 20 feet away from him. He reacted by grabbing Luke Daab in a chokehold and using him as a shield.

Dad fired the neuron gun. The discharge would stun all of the neuron pathways in both Dr. Jordan and Luke Daab, hurting them both but not damaging either of them permanently.

Nothing happened.

Dr. Jordan grinned evilly at Dad, turning his round face into a pucker of satisfied smugness.

Then I understood.

The neuron gun could only operate under two conditions. The fingerprints of the person holding the gun had to match the computer instructions in the neuron gun's microchip. And activation had to be permitted by the mainframe computer.

If Dr. Jordan was somehow controlling the mainframe, he would have also disabled the neuron gun.

Dad fired again. Then he must have realized the same thing I did.

I felt Ashley bump up against me.

The three of us against Dr. Jordan. We still had a

chance, even without the neuron gun. Four of us, if Luke Daab could get out of the chokehold.

"Back away!" Dr. Jordan shouted. We were close enough that we could barely hear him above the siren. Light bounced off his round glasses, hiding his eyes from us. "I'll snap his neck like a chicken bone!"

To emphasize his threat, Dr. Jordan squeezed the chokehold harder with his right forearm and began to turn Luke Daab's head with his left hand. Pain and fear filled the small janitor's face.

Dad stopped.

Dr. Jordan smiled coldly. "Good-bye!" he shouted. "I know you've been looking for a bomb. Too bad you didn't think computer bomb, because the chain of events I started on your mainframe is going to be very interesting! Start putting on your suntan lotion!"

With those final words, he pulled Luke Daab into the escape pod.

The hatch slid shut behind them.

And 20 seconds later the escape pod ejected from the ship.

CHAPTER 21

I stared at points of light through the clear wall of the navigation cone. Only in my imagination could I wonder if I saw sunlight gleaming off the escape pod. Even though only half an hour had passed, it was thousands of miles away.

"It doesn't make me feel better that I was right in my guess," Dad said. A blip on his monitor showed the location of the escape pod. "Jordan's using the momentum of the ship for a slingshot effect. Add our current speed to the speed of the pod's ejection from the ship, plus the burst of acceleration from its own fuel supply and the escape pod has effectively doubled our speed. Which means they . . ."

It took Dad a few seconds to make his calculation. "They'll be in orbit range of Earth in 10 days. And we're not scheduled to arrive for almost three weeks."

"Wrong." Lance Evenson had dropped from the travel tube into the navigation cone.

"Wrong?" Dad repeated.

"Wrong," he said, frowning. "But let me give you all the good news first. That radio signal you want me to send ahead with news about his escape? Except for an emergency beacon, our mainframe won't permit any communications. In or out of the ship. It's part of the preprogramming that was coded into the mainframe without our authorization."

"That's the good news?" Dad said.

"Sure," Lance said in a voice heavy with sarcasm. "Plus the fact that I still can't break the computer code that has locked down all the hatches. Everyone is still stuck in their bunkers with no access to food or water."

"Any more good news?"

"Unless you want me to let you know that I did find a wire from the mainframe to an infrared antenna in the ceiling panel halfway down the corridor. Which means whoever did the new programming had as much time as they wanted to make it foolproof. Which means I'm not sure I can break the new code soon enough. Unless I find the computer that wrote that code."

"Soon enough?"

Lance shook his head. "Sure. Now I get to tell you the bad news. Our ion engine is burning fuel at a tremendous rate. Remember the acceleration jolt we felt just before the siren went off?"

Dad nodded.

"Mainframe again. Instructing the engine to go into overdrive. Our engine is set at maximum and, with every 30 minutes that passes, we're picking up speed at the rate of 1,000 miles an hour. By tomorrow, we'll be close to 50,000 miles an hour faster than we are now. With that much speed, we'll probably pass the escape pod before it's halfway to Earth."

Looking out through the navigation cone gave me no sense of the speed of our ship. Unlike on the surface of Mars—where the nearby boulders served as reference points and even 20 miles an hour seemed fast because of

102

it—here in space the nearest reference points were billions of miles away. It took days to see any shift, so it never felt like we were moving.

"Lance, you've got to slow this down," Dad said. "With that kind of speed, hitting a pebble could blow us apart. And—" He stopped as his face suddenly went blank.

"Exactly," Lance said. "Getting blown apart might be the best we could hope for."

"What?" I asked. "If we don't hit anything, what can be so bad about reaching Earth's orbit so soon? We'll even beat Dr. Jordan there and be able to wait for him and save Luke Daab."

"We'll reach Earth's orbit," Lance agreed. Quietly. "And then blow through it and past it."

"Tyce," Dad added, "at the beginning of a space journey like this, fuel is burned to accelerate us to maximum safe speed. Once we're at that speed, we coast with no friction to slow us down. Some fuel is burned in the middle for slight adjustments in the flight course. And if the calculations are done right, there's enough fuel left at the end of the journey to put the engine in a reverse thrust and slow us down. That's space travel. Gradual acceleration. Followed by gradual deceleration. With just enough fuel loaded to take care of both."

Did that mean what I thought it meant?

Dad continued. "Our fuel margins are thin anyway. We build in about a 10 percent error rate. What's happening now is that every hour of fuel we burn puts us in double jeopardy. It's an extra hour of gained speed and one less hour of fuel to slow us down. Lance, have you done the rest of the calculations?"

"Yes. And that's the worst news I can deliver."

"I'd rather know it now," Dad said.

I wasn't sure if I wanted to hear it.

"If I can't find a way to break the programming code sometime in the next two hours," Lance told us, "we may have gained too much speed. Burning what remains of our fuel with the reverse thruster after that will only slow us down to a couple thousand miles per hour. And then no more fuel. There will be nothing left to bring us to a stop. And you know how it is in space. We'll just keep coasting at that speed."

At a couple thousand miles per hour. Forever?

"And what if you can't break the programming code at all?" Dad asked.

"We continue accelerating until the fuel is gone. We pass the Earth at over 100,000 miles per hour. Headed straight toward the sun."

That's what Dr. Jordan meant when he told us to start putting on suntan lotion. He knew exactly what had been planned.

Dad closed his eyes, then opened them. He spoke very calmly. "What you're saying is that in two hours, even if the computer lets us start communicating with anyone on Earth, there is no way any orbit shuttle would be able to catch or stop this ship as it flew past."

"That's exactly what I'm saying," Lance agreed. "We're only going to live as long as our food supplies last. Unless we hit the sun first."

CHAPTER 22

Diabolical.

That's the only way I can describe it.

Diabolical.

I'm not even sure there is any point in writing any of this into my diary. After all, who will ever be able to read it when my comp-board and everything else on this ship burns down to a collection of atoms and molecules spewed out of the sun?

Or maybe we'll miss the sun and head to the outer reaches of the solar system, then beyond. Our ship will be lifeless, carrying only skeletons. And it's not likely that anyone would ever find this ghost ship and read my diary.

All because of that diabolical Dr. Jordan.

By getting into the mainframe, he had set the ship's engine on maximum burn. If that wasn't enough, he'd blocked our communications systems so that we couldn't radio for help or send a message explaining how he'd doomed the ship. And if that wasn't enough insurance to make sure no one lived, Dr. Jordan had the computer close

down every hatch so that everyone would be
trapped in their bunkers. Only because Dad had
reacted quickly and instinctively did that final part
of Dr. Jordan's plan fail. Well, at least with Dr.
Jordan now escaped, I don't have to worry about
someone logging on to my comp-board.

In the silence and privacy of my own bunker, I stopped
keyboarding.

Almost two hours had passed since our discussion in
the navigation cone. Long enough for Dad to manually
break open every hatch door and let everyone out and tell
them the bad news. And long enough for us to pass the
point of no return. Now, even if Lance regained control of
the mainframe, we didn't have enough fuel to bring the ship
to a stop. Now, even if we could start the communications
system, an SOS for help would do no good. We were traveling too fast for any military ship to rescue us.

SOS.

When I'd asked, Dad had explained that SOS meant
"save our souls," a plea from sinking ships when the
ancient technology of wireless telegraph meant messages
had to be sent by something called Morse code.

Save our souls.

Believe it or not, Blaine Steven, stuck behind with the
rest of us, had actually started praying with Dad. Funny how
the thought of death makes a person also think of God.
Especially a person I'd assumed would never be faintly
interested in God.

And Lance Evenson?

He'd told us the rest of the story behind the disc in his
air vent. How from the beginning of his time on Mars he'd
allowed an unknown someone access to the Mars Dome's

mainframe. It had been ridiculously simple, he'd explained. All it took was giving that person the access code.

Why? Dad had asked.

Money, Lance had explained. Enough retirement money that when he returned to Earth, he would have no worries. He'd thought that taking all the information, including the security override program, with him on the disc would be insurance in case someone found out what he did and tried to blackmail him.

Who? Dad had asked.

That was just it, Lance had answered. He never knew. The money went into a bank account on Earth with regular payments that he could check with E-mail requests from Mars. All Lance knew was that it had to be someone on Mars who had also been there from the beginning. And that this unknown person had access to a computer that tapped into the Mars Dome mainframe. Just like he'd done it on this spaceship.

I read from the beginning of what I had typed.

One sentence stuck out.

Well, at least with Dr. Jordan now escaped, I don't have to worry about someone logging on to my comp-board.

Why had I assumed I didn't have to worry about it anymore? It wasn't Dr. Jordan who had logged on to my comp-board. He didn't have any access to a computer in his prison bunker. No. He'd been cabled to the wall, just like Blaine Steven. Any access that Dr. Jordan did have could only have happened during the midnight-to-early-morning hours when he was out of his bunker, as shown by the computer's activity log of the hatch openings to his prison bunker.

Someone else on this ship had helped him get in and out of his bunker. Was that person still on the ship?

No, I decided, *definitely not.* Because the computer had slammed shut all the hatches, trapping everyone in their bunkers. And because the computer had programmed the engine and communications system to make sure everyone remaining on the ship would die sooner or later. Whoever had helped Dr. Jordan would do his or her best not to be on the ship when the escape pod ejected.

But the only person off the ship right now with Dr. Jordan was Luke Daab.

In all that had happened since their escape, none of us had questioned why Dr. Jordan had taken a hostage with him. That was one extra person to use food and water on the escape pod. Dr. Jordan didn't need a hostage if everyone left behind on the ship was going to die anyway. Unless Luke Daab wasn't a hostage.

Luke Daab. The same Luke Daab who had made it possible for Dr. Jordan to ask Ashley about her escape from the Hammerhead space torpedo?

Now I knew why Dr. Jordan had wanted to know. To make sure Ashley didn't have some unexpected way of getting out of the *Moon Racer.* Or some unexpected way of rescuing all of us.

But Luke Daab?

Images flashed into my mind. Luke in the computer room, with wall panels out and wiring exposed. Luke in the corridor, with ceiling panels out and wiring exposed. Luke Daab, working wherever he wanted on the ship, almost invisible to people who passed by him.

A maintenance engineer could come and go anywhere on the ship without ever being questioned. Just like a maintenance engineer could come and go anywhere under the dome without ever being questioned. The same maintenance engineer who had been under the Mars Dome since it had been first established.

Luke Daab?

Another image flashed into my mind. Of Luke shouting something as Ashley and Dad and I had rushed down the corridor and first met them about to enter the escape pod. Something we couldn't hear above the noise of the wailing siren. I had assumed he was shouting to us. What if he had been shouting to Dr. Jordan?

If Luke was the mastermind behind all of this, maybe he was commanding Dr. Jordan to make it look like a hostage situation. Commanding Dr. Jordan to put a chokehold on him and fool us.

But why?

If Luke had set it up so that we were all going to die anyhow, why would he want us to think he was a helpless victim? So that Dad wouldn't shoot them with the neuron gun?

No. The mainframe had already been programmed to shut the neuron gun down. Luke and Dr. Jordan knew that. They weren't afraid of the neuron gun.

So that we wouldn't tackle them? No, by the time we got there, they were close enough to jump into the escape pod before we could close the gap.

Then why go to the pretense of making it look like a hostage situation?

When the answer hit me, I shouted out loud.

Then raced to find Dad.

CHAPTER 23

"Here! I found it!"

Dad's voice rang inside the walls of Luke Daab's bunker.

There were three of us. Dad. Ashley. Me. All of us pulling away wall and ceiling panels to find what Luke Daab might have hidden.

Until now, we only had his personal comp-board, which he had left behind the netting of a storage shelf. But a comp-board had nowhere near the power needed to crunch out the code needed to override the mainframe. Which was what I had guessed only 10 minutes earlier while keyboarding my latest diary entry.

"And it's got an infrared antenna," Dad continued. He pointed to a small computer hard drive nestled into a compartment behind a wall panel. "So he could not only link wireless to the mainframe but also to his comp-board. It's the go-between computer. It could intercept anything—even Rawling's *real* E-mails to you. You were right, Tyce. If Luke decided not take this with him, he sure wouldn't want us finding it. With any luck, Lance can use this hard drive to regain control of the mainframe."

"Yes and no," Lance reported to Dad a half hour later. Ashley and I had waited in the navigation cone with Dad, each of us hardly speaking because of the nervous tension.

"Yes, I've regained control of the mainframe," Lance continued. "And no. The communications system is totally disabled. As are the controls to the flaps and reverse thruster."

"But if you've got the mainframe back . . ."

Lance laughed sourly. "The guy's a genius. And very, very cautious. As if he anticipated the one-in-a-thousand chance we'd find his computer setup in his bunker. He programmed the mainframe alarm system to be silenced so that it would seem like everything on board the ship was normal. But it isn't."

"I don't like the sound of this," Dad said.

"You shouldn't," Lance answered. "Luke Daab wrecked the communications systems and piloting controls the old-fashioned way. With a hammer."

"With a hammer!" It was as if Lance had slapped Dad's face.

Lance nodded. "He was the maintenance engineer. Always carried his tool belt. Had the perfect excuse to be wherever he wanted on the ship. Sometime in the last day or two he took a hammer to the physical components of the systems. Just like he destroyed all the vital computer parts of the second escape pod to make sure we couldn't eject it if somehow we regained control of the mainframe. Normally, the mainframe would clang out alarm bells louder than a fire alarm as soon as it detected the malfunction. But with the computer programmed to ignore the malfunction signals . . ."

"We've got nothing, then. We're stuck on a ship with no communications and no manual piloting controls."

"All I was able to do was reduce the burn rate of our fuel to nothing, for now. We've stopped accelerating. Even so, if we don't figure out a way to start slowing down in the next hour, we'll shoot too far past the Earth for our emergency beacon to reach anyone."

"So if we are somehow able to start slowing down right away," Ashley said, "someone might come looking?"

"If we stop." Dad swung in his chair to face her squarely. "And if we stop close enough to the orbital shipping lanes between Earth and Mars. Neither possibility gives us much hope."

I hadn't spoken since Lance had entered the navigation cone. "There is," I said, "one tiny chance."

All of them stared at me.

"Hey," I finished, "the big 'bots' are still in the cargo bay, aren't they?"

CHAPTER 24

Darkness.

Since I wasn't receiving the light signals through human eyes, waiting wasn't going to help my vision adjust. But that didn't matter. I knew that within moments light from the stars and sun would flood the inside of the cargo bay.

I heard a muted clank as the lock released. Then a hiss as the vacuum of outer space sucked all of the air out of the cargo bay. That was the last sound I could expect to hear. Sound does not travel in a vacuum, and the cargo bay slowly swung open to expose my robot body to the open solar system.

Light entered. The light of millions of galaxies and billions of stars, so diamond clear that I felt a thrill of incredible joy.

There was movement beside me.

The other robot, controlled by Ashley. Like me, she was hooked by remote to a computer hard drive in the robot center inside the *Moon Racer*.

The robot waved. I waved back.

She had a newer model, but both were constructed with similar designs.

The lower body of the robot is much like my wheelchair. Instead of a pair of legs, an axle connects two wheels. On land, just like a wheelchair, it turns by moving one wheel forward while the other wheel remains motionless or moves backward.

The robot's upper body is a short, thick, hollow pole that sticks through the axle, with a heavy weight to counter-balance the arms and head. Within this weight is the battery that powers the robot, with wires running up inside the hollow pole.

At the upper end of the pole is a crosspiece to which arms are attached. The arms swing freely without hitting the wheels. Like the rest of the robot, they are made of titanium and are jointed like human arms, with one difference. All the joints swivel. The hands, too, are like human hands, but with only three fingers and a thumb instead of four fingers and a thumb.

Four video lenses at the top of the pole serve as eyes. One faces forward, one backward, and one to each side.

Three tiny microphones, attached to the underside of the video lenses, play the role of ears, taking in sound. The fourth speaker, underneath the video lens that faces forward, produces sound and allows us to make our voices heard.

The computer drive is well protected within the hollow titanium pole that serves as the robot's upper body. Since it's mounted on shock absorbers, the robot can fall 10 feet without shaking the computer drive. This computer drive has a short antenna plug at the back of the pole to send and receive X-ray signals.

Both of our robots held a handjet in their right hand to allow us to propel the robots through space. My own robot held a welder's torch in the left hand. Ashley's robot held eight narrow strips of metal, all of them about two feet long. All of this had been placed in the cargo bay before Ashley and I had started the control sequence.

I waved one more time, then pointed at the open cargo door.

Her robot waved back and nodded.

I pushed forward. We had work to do.

The cargo bay had an inner door, which sealed the *Moon Racer* from outer space while the outer door was open. For humans who had to return to the inside of the *Moon Racer*, this was important. On their return from space the outer door would be closed and sealed, then the inner door opened, allowing air back into the cargo bay. Without the outer door closed again, it would be suicide for everyone in the *Moon Racer* to open the inner door.

For robots, however, it didn't matter. Not if they didn't ever need to get inside the *Moon Racer.* That simple fact was the only chance of survival for everyone else.

Because what we had to do would mean destroying the outer wide, flat cargo door.

I hit a propellant button on my handjet and pushed toward the cargo door.

Ashley followed. Each robot was attached to the wall of the cargo bay by hundreds of yards of thin cable that would prevent it from being lost in space.

Near the hinges of the cargo door, I stopped. I was now half inside the cargo bay and half outside, with the door wide open. I looked down at my wheels. Below, nothingness stretched to infinity.

It was not the time to enjoy a view, however. I clicked the button that fired up the welder's torch.

Ashley and I had gone over this a dozen times inside the spaceship. She knew what her robot had to do. I knew my robot's job. I nodded one more time to let her know I was ready.

She tucked her own handjet under the robot arm so both hands were free.

My handjet was off, and I used it to tap a spot on the edge of the door near the lower hinge.

Immediately Ashley's robot placed the end of one of the metal strips against the spot I had touched. Her robot held it there while I welded it on. The weld cooled almost instantly in the black chill of space. I handed her robot the torch and bent the strip upward, then back down, so that it formed an upside-down *U*. I took the torch from her robot and welded the other end of the strip in place. We had formed our first bracket.

We did it again, a little higher. The two brackets were now a shoulder-width apart.

Then we moved outward, staying with the door. At the opposite end of the door, near the latch that would hold it in place when it was shut, my robot body hung motionless, with infinity stretching in all directions.

But it was still no time to enjoy the view. Or even to marvel at the fact that we clung to a spaceship moving at thousands upon thousands of miles per hour but, without air around us, we didn't seem to be moving at all.

On this end of the door, I welded one bracket on, then another. These two were also a shoulder-width apart, roughly parallel with the two on the other side. Now we had four primitive handholds permanently attached to the inner side of the door.

Aware of how important it was to move quickly, I pointed at the last two brackets. Ashley's robot nodded and handed me the remaining four strips of metal. I bent them in a rough circle around the edge of one of my robot wheels. I nodded again.

Her robot grabbed a bracket in each hand and hung there from the outer edge of the door, as if hanging from a handhold in the corridor of the *Moon Racer.* Her robot remained there while I used my handjet to move back to the hinges. Without hesitation, using the incredible heat of the welding torch in my other hand, I cut the hinges loose. The door fell away from the *Moon Racer.*

With Ashley's robot still hanging from the brackets, I guided the door through the weightlessness of outer space, back toward the ion thruster of the *Moon Racer.*

We were halfway done.

The ion thruster was simply a giant nozzle that directed a stream of propelling ions into space. If Lance had not been able to turn down the fuel-burn ratio earlier, our plan would not have had a chance.

As it was, it would still be tricky.

When we arrived, I used my handjet to push the wheels of Ashley's robot against the outer wall of the giant nozzle. I took one of the strips of metal I'd wrapped around my own robot wheels and bent it into another *U*. I turned the *U* upside down and put it between the spokes of one of her robot wheels. I welded one end to the outer wall of the thruster, then the other. I had just bracketed her robot permanently into place. I did the same with her other wheel.

All of this happened in slow-motion ballet. Movements in outer space have to be smooth and even, something I had learned the hard way during virtual-reality sessions. I wished it could go faster, but I had to get it right the first time.

It did look strange.

Her robot was now attached by its wheels to the outside of the thruster nozzle. And its hands held the brackets I had welded on the cargo door.

Three-quarters of the way there.

I left Ashley's robot there and pushed around to the opposite side of the ion thruster. With the final two strips of metal, I welded *U*-shaped strips around my own wheels so that my robot, too, was permanently attached to the outside of the thruster nozzle.

I waved at Ashley's robot on the other side of the nozzle. It was weird, thinking that each of these robot bodies moved because of the brain-wave impulses that Ashley and I were sending to computers inside the *Moon Racer.* And weird to think that very soon Ashley and I would wake up inside the robot room, with these two robots remaining out here, doing a highly unexpected job. *If* my plan worked.

I nodded one final time and watched as her robot began to swing the door down toward the opening of the thruster. Had there been ions streaming out, it would have blown the door backward like a flap in the wind. Instead, her robot was able to lower the door until my robot could reach out and grab the handhold brackets on the opposite side.

Just like that, we were finished.

Now there was a robot on each side, holding the door like an umbrella, just a few feet above the nozzle of the ion thruster.

CHAPTER 25

"Ready?" Dad asked Lance.

"As ready as we'll ever be," he replied.

Ashley and I crowded behind Dad as he watched the monitor with Lance. Everyone else was in the entertainment cluster, waiting just as anxiously as we were.

"Then fire it up," Dad said. "We need to start as soon as possible. My calculations show we'll barely make it as it is."

If it works, I thought.

Lance rapidly keyboarded some commands.

For several seconds, nothing happened.

"Is the fuel-burn ratio up?" Dad asked anxiously.

Lance pointed at the computer screen. "That's what it says. But it always takes a bit of time for the ions to—"

Bang!

The *Moon Racer* lurched, throwing us to the side.

All of us hit the opposite wall as the *Moon Racer* suddenly slowed.

And we began to cheer! Other cheers reached us from the corridor. The others, too, understood we had just felt sudden deceleration.

It had worked.

The cargo door was now funneling the ions in the same way that a reverse thruster would!

Dad hugged me. I hugged Ashley. Lance hugged all three of us.

"All right," Dad said. "Lance, monitor it closely. But thanks to Tyce and Ashley's quick work to help us slow down and the fuel we have left, we should get this thing almost to a standstill by the time we reach Earth. And with the emergency locator, someone will find us soon enough."

Lance's big grin faded.

"I know. I know," Dad said. "And then you'll face arrest when we get Earth-side. But with all that you've done now and if you testify against Dr. Jordan and Luke Daab, I don't think it will be as bad as you expect. And I'll do whatever I can to help."

Trouble was, almost three weeks later, when the soldiers of a military rescue shuttle boarded the ship, the first people arrested were Dad and me.

EPILOGUE

03.27.2040

Of all my dreams about Earth, I never expected I would get here and not see anything except four walls of a prison cell. I now know the true definition of misery. My body aches. After a lifetime of gravity at only one-third of the planet Earth's, my bones feel heavy, my muscles weak, and my lungs tired. At all of the points where my body sits in my wheelchair, my skin is raw from the unaccustomed weight and pressure. I can't imagine how much worse this would have been if I hadn't been working out daily during the trip from Mars to Earth.

Dad said it would take a week at least to adjust to the new gravity, but I wonder if I ever will.

As for my dreams about all the different foods I'd be able to try, those too have become a nightmare. Prison food is horrible.

I don't know exactly where I am, just that it's some windowless room the size of a closet, and that it has been two days since our arrests.

I haven't seen my dad. Or Ashley. And I'm not sure what happened to them or the others because we were arrested so quickly. All I have is my comp-board, and even all of its files were searched, copied, and transferred before I could keep it.

So now I'm writing my diary in case Dad or Mom or Rawling ever gets ahold of this.

All I can do is hope. . . .

I stopped keyboarding at the sound of scratching on my prison door. It sounded like the guard's keys. Which meant I would get yet another rotten meal.

It wasn't a guard.

But a robot!

"Hello," a familiar voice said from the robot's speakers. "You all right, Tyce?"

"Ashley? Ashley!" I called out to the robot.

I pushed forward, expecting that I would float through the air in her direction. Nothing happened. I was on Earth, not in the freedom and weightlessness of space.

"Shhh!" she said anxiously. "We only have about five minutes."

"For what?" I asked.

"What else?" she said. "Escape. You and I have a lot to do before all of this is over."

WILL COMPUTERS SOMEDAY REPLACE MAN?

Computers already surround us. And in the future, they'll become even more important. Just look at Tyce Sanders's world, where Lance Evenson, the chief computer technician, is the most important person on the *Moon Racer*! After all, he's the guy who keeps all the computers running on this intergalactic 2040 spaceship.

But you know what? This mission shows that all the technology in the world can't match our human ingenuity. When the computer system is useless, Tyce's creativity—using the robots to slow down the *Moon Racer*—is what saves the spaceship from shooting past Earth into deep, black nothingness. Tyce's dad's quick, instinctive reactions keep the hatch door from locking them in. And Tyce even has to "rescue" the ant-bot by knotting threads from a regulation jumpsuit to fish the robot out of the air vent. I guess robots aren't so smart after all!

Humans created robots and computers, and that's why they have problems. It's because we humans aren't perfect, either. Although we are created by God, in his image, he gives us a choice: Will we follow him and his ways or not?

Some people, like Blaine Steven, count on technology and power to get what they want. But such things can't save them from possible death. When ex-director Steven thought he might die, all of a sudden he began to ask Tyce questions about faith and God. Tyce was shocked, because Steven seemed like somebody who'd *never* want to know— or care—about religion.

But appearances can be deceiving. Tyce found that out the hard way. He had accused Lance Evenson, who looked like a tough guy, of being the mastermind behind the plot. When all the time it was actually weak and drab Luke Daab who fooled them all.

We humans look at appearances, but God looks at the heart. Because God loves us, he encourages us to make right decisions. Why? Because he knows bad decisions can effect us for a lifetime and he hurts when we hurt. He also knows that such a lifestyle drives us away from him.

Can you ever do something so wrong that God will never take you back?

Now that my wife, Cindy, and I have a daughter, Olivia, I understand even more fully the promises that Jesus made to us as humans. No matter what lifestyle decisions Olivia might ever make down the road, no matter how far away from us she might go, all she would have to do is turn around and reach out for us, and we would take her back with joy.

The same is true with God and his love for us. No matter how far we might stray from him, he is always waiting with love and hope for our return. (Just read the parable of the Prodigal Son for proof!)

When Jesus walked this world, he had an incredible message. You see, the religious leaders of his time taught that in order to approach God and be with him, you had to first make yourself right by paying penalties for what you had done wrong. Jesus said it was the opposite. All you need to do is approach God through his Son, Jesus, admit your wrongs, and ask for forgiveness. Then God will enter your life and transform it, giving you hope, peace, and joy for the future. Then, when life on this Earth is over, you'll find your real home. In heaven. In God's love.

And that's something only humans can experience—not computers.

ABOUT THE AUTHOR

Sigmund Brouwer, his wife, recording artist Cindy Morgan, and their daughter split living between Red Deer, Alberta, Canada, and Nashville, Tennessee. He has written several series of juvenile fiction and eight novels. Sigmund loves sports and plays golf and hockey. He also enjoys visiting schools to talk about books. He welcomes visitors to his Web site at www.coolreading.com, where he and a bunch of other authors like to hang out in cyberspace.